"IF YOU REALLY WANT TO SHOW YOUR APPRECIATION..."

His strong hands came up to grasp her shoulders and pull her tight against him, letting her feel the warmth of his body. An instant later, his mouth captured hers in a ruthless and searching kiss.

She stiffened as the kiss hardened and probed, trying to keep her lips tight against the sensuous onslaught. He gave her an angry shake, and murmured, "Dammit! Don't tell me you need lessons in how to kiss a man!"

Red-hot anger made her open her lips to protest and it was all the opportunity he needed. He kissed her again and she didn't have a chance to resist. Under his expert persuasion, her last thought of resistance melted away, and when they gravitated to the soft cushions of the nearby couch, *it was by mutual agreement. . . .*

More SIGNET Books by Glenna Finley

Love's Temptation

Temptation

Glenna Finley

*The only way to get rid of a temptation
is to yield to it.*

—*Wilde*

A SIGNET BOOK
NEW AMERICAN LIBRARY
TIMES MIRROR

Ⓢ

SIGNET TRADEMARK REG. U.S. PAT. OFF. AND FOREIGN COUNTRIES
REGISTERED TRADEMARK—MARCA REGISTRADA
HECHO EN CHICAGO, U.S.A.

SIGNET, SIGNET CLASSICS, MENTOR, PLUME AND MERIDIAN BOOKS
are published by The New American Library, Inc.,
1301 Avenue of the Americas, New York, New York 10019

First Printing, December, 1979

1 2 3 4 5 6 7 8 9

PRINTED IN THE UNITED STATES OF AMERICA

Chapter

–1–

Lucinda Forsythe heard the disparaging snort as she walked by the corral. She took a minute to stop and survey the piebald colt standing on the other side of the fence before saying, "I don't know what's so funny. Frankly, you're nothing to write home about either. If I'd had my way, neither one of us would have even a nodding acquaintance."

The horse gazed back at her, snuffled disdainfully again, and turned his attention to a clump of grass.

"So much for western hospitality," Lucie muttered as she switched her attention then to the majestic Grand Teton range, looming behind the Jackson Lake resort. She was impressed and captivated by the peaks which formed such a spectacular backdrop to the Wyoming scenery. Although it was only the middle of September, an early storm had already sifted snow onto the mountaintops and partway down the rocky sides. The snow was the only evidence of autumn's arrival, however; the grasses on the valley floor were still brown from the summer sun and leaves clung stubbornly to the birch trees on the resort grounds.

At any other time, Lucie would have viewed her

1

surroundings with a sense of well-being if not outright enthusiasm. As it was, she turned back to the horse browsing on the other side of the fence and addressed it with some bitterness. "At least *your* relatives have the good sense to leave you alone instead of insisting of a 'togetherness' routine. My own mother should know that I'm too old to be falling on a stranger's neck. But now that she's married this man's father, she's decided that we're going to be one big happy family."

Lucie sighed and leaned against the fence, thoroughly annoyed by the circumstances which brought about her reluctant appearance in Wyoming. A ranch resort, no matter how luxurious, wasn't her natural habitat—or even her chosen one. At age twenty-three, she had firmly decided that she was a woman who preferred city life. More specifically, life within the city limits of San Francisco. A trip to the neighboring Monterey peninsula was as close to "country" as she deigned to get.

Her acquaintances could go backpacking and birdwatching all they chose. Lucie's birdwatching was done in comfort at the zoo on sunny days as she hiked happily to the aviary. Her chosen weekend locales included tennis courts and swimming pools. The latter, preferably heated. She had an excellent job as a buyer in the fur salon of an exclusive department store, which materialized after she obtained a college degree in business and retail merchandising. Subsequent promotions had been rapid, and she hoped that they occurred because of her grasp of business problems. Only occasionally did she suspect that her progress might have been attributed to a size-ten figure which curved in all the right places, and other similar feminine assets.

By then, the piebald colt behind the fence was ignoring her, but it was one of the few times that any male had done so since she'd shed her braces some years before. Men don't often overlook women whose dark brown hair gleams with tawny highlights—like the rich shade of sable. Or the possessors of intelligent hazel eyes, smooth complexions, and lips which curve appealingly most of the time. If there was any drawback to Lucie's profile, it was a chin which could, occasionally, be amazingly determined.

Even that determination had been to no avail after the wedding, when her mother and brand new stepfather had insisted that she detour on her vacation to meet her stepfather's son and bring him up to date on the event since he'd been unable to attend the ceremony.

It was Lucie's private opinion that if Drew McLaren couldn't rearrange his business affairs for such an occasion, he really didn't deserve any consideration afterward.

She'd already gleaned that Drew could do little wrong in his father's eyes. "It isn't the boy's fault that those damned negotiations are dragging on," McLaren senior had announced. He'd gone on to tell Lucie's mother, "Drew insists we have the ceremony performed without him. After all, he has plenty of time to get to know his new family."

But after the nuptials, the newlyweds decided that Lucie shouldn't waste a minute in getting to know "the boy"—an absurd name for a man already on the shady side of thirty.

Although the name might be apt after all, Lucie thought. Everybody knew that an only son tended to be immature and indulged. If she'd been more logical in her thoughts, she would have remembered that the "only child" description fitted her equally well. Just then, however, she wasn't seeing things in her normal way.

Since the McLaren family owned a resort ranch in Arizona, it wasn't surprising that Drew would choose a similar locale to meet his new relation. At least that's what Lucie had thought until her stepfather had set her right at the airport. "Nice of you to fall in with Drew's plans," he'd said before he and Lucie's mother had gotten on a plane to Hawaii for their honeymoon. "He wanted to look over the gift shop operation at the Jackson Lodge and thought he might as well do it now. Besides, it'll be good for you to practice your horseback riding. Your mother and I want you to spend your spare time at our place from now on."

Lucie, who had no intention of imposing on their newly-wedded status, started to protest, and then subsided as she saw her mother's anxious expression. She swallowed a hot reply, managing instead to say, "That's nice of you. I'll have to see what happens. Actually the store doesn't give me much time off." Which was certainly true enough.

So here she was, wasting two days of her precious holiday staring at horses and shivering in a Wyoming breeze when she might have been working on a suntan farther south.

Earlier, she'd felt guilty about her lack of enthusiasm and called the corral for a riding appointment. After all, she told herself sternly, if she was going to see her parents even on periodic visits in the future, she'd have to be able to look at a horse without shuddering. She'd disliked riding ever since a pony had run away with her at the seashore when she was a child. Lucie could imagine what the McLaren family reaction would be to that story! Possibly Drew would suggest that she see a psychiatrist before her next visit and avoid anything with four legs in the meantime.

That thought made her frown again. Probably Drew McLaren was convinced by now that his new stepmother was a widow who'd been on the prowl for a nicely bankrolled husband. He'd never believe that it took all sorts of persuasion from Lucie before her shy mother would even consider another marriage proposal. Supremely happy in her first marriage, she'd had no thoughts about finding a successor. Hamish McLaren, too, had been a widower for years and content with his life until he'd taken one look at the gentle and attractive woman sitting beside him at a dinner party and set about persuading her to be his wife.

If Lucie hadn't been a successful and independent young woman, her mother wouldn't have considered remarriage, and even the day before the ceremony, she had to be assured that Hamish's only offspring was equally content with the impending nuptials.

Which was as it should be, Lucie reasoned. It was impossible to mistake her mother for anything but the sweet and unassuming woman that she was. However, it was a pity that Drew couldn't attend the wedding and find out for himself. That way, the newlyweds would have been satisfied, leaving Drew and Lucie to go on with their own affairs.

Figuratively speaking, of course, Lucie concluded. At least as far as she was concerned. From the little she knew of Drew McLaren, his interest in the feminine sex apparently came lower on the list than the McLaren business empire. "Otherwise he certainly could have postponed his miserable negotiations," she muttered aloud.

"I beg your pardon?" came a startled masculine voice close by.

Lucie turned quickly, appalled to find a stranger on the path beside her. He was an exceptionally good-looking man of average height. His olive skin, combined with dark hair and eyes, indicated a Mediterranean ancestor not far back in his family tree. He was wearing jeans and a denim jacket, but he didn't appear particularly comfortable in casual garb. Even more incongruous was his white silk shirt. Lucie decided that he really needed a cashmere suit to go along with that item and tried to conceal her amusement as she met his inquiring glance.

"I guess I was talking to myself," she said with a rueful smile. "At least, I didn't expect an answer. It's been one-sided, so far." She gestured toward the piebald colt who gave them a cursory appraisal and went back to his grazing.

"Obviously he hasn't been around much," the man replied, showing no inclination to leave. "If you're walking back to the lodge, I'll keep you company."

He jerked his head toward the big building a scant half mile away at the end of the curving drive. "Maybe by the time we get there, you'd even let me buy you a drink. Incidentally, my name's Victor Perelli—Vito to my friends."

It was impossible to take offense at his forthright manner, and Lucie's smile widened in response. "I'm Lucinda Forsythe."

"Lucinda," he echoed, his deep voice giving resonance to the consonants. "I like it. Now, about that drink—" He broke off as he saw her start to shake her head. "Can't you make it?"

"I'm sorry," she said and meant it. "I have an appointment. Up there." She nodded toward a small building by the corral gate.

"With a horse?" Vito sounded incredulous. "You don't look like the type. I thought I'd finally found a soul mate." Before she could get the wrong idea, he added, "Most of the people at this place look as if they'd come into the world in a bronc chute instead of a hospital."

"You mean I don't pass?" Lucie asked in mock dismay, glancing at her own jeans and checked shirt. "The clerk at the shop in the lodge practically guaranteed I'd fit right in."

Vito's black eyebrows climbed. "I noticed the difference right away. You'll have to switch that French perfume for Fels Naphtha if you want to join the other bunch. Can't you change your mind about the drink?"

She shook her head regretfully.

"What about later?" he inquired. "You could always wander by the cocktail lounge before dinner."

"I'd better wait and see," Lucie told him, not wishing to bare her soul and confess that she probably wouldn't be able to sit down at dinnertime if the riding session went as predicted.

"Maybe tomorrow?" Vito asked, hopefully.

"Tomorrow I'm expecting to meet someone."

"I knew it." He frowned. "That just leaves tonight. If I make a dining room reservation for seven, how about meeting me in the lobby. If you're earlier, I'll be in the bar. I refuse to miss my chances with the only woman who doesn't look like a barrel draped in denim."

"All right, dinner will be fine, thanks," Lucie agreed, deciding that it would be fun to share a table with such a presentable man. At least it would take her mind off meeting Drew McLaren the next day— an event which didn't thrill her any more than the forthcoming riding lesson. That thought brought her mind back to the present and she gasped as she looked at her watch. "Oh, Lord—I'm late now. I'll have to go."

"Okay. I'll find you later."

"I may be limping," she warned.

He grinned, obviously pleased with the way things had turned out. "Gin can double as linament in an emergency. Tell the Lone Ranger up there to give you a short trip." He winked and strode back along the path toward the lodge.

Lucie didn't waste any time looking after him. Instead, she set off toward the corral, hoping that she wasn't too late for her appointment.

When she arrived at the hut a minute or so later, it appeared that she needn't have hurried. Aside from a spider busily enlarging a web in the corner of the rough-lumbered room, she was in sole possession of the premises. True, there was a counter with a telephone on it and a list with her name at the top. That showed some employee had been around earlier— unless the piebald colt did double duty.

She stepped outside again and surveyed the corral. After girding herself for the damned horseback ride, she intended to carry through. Somewhere, there must be a person who fed, curried, or cleaned up after the string of horses standing by the fence.

At that moment, two men appeared from behind some baled straw stacked down to her left. To Lucie's annoyance, they ignored her completely and continued their conversation, standing in the shade of a timbered shed.

The seconds went by while Lucie's temper rose, matching the sun's heat on her uncovered head as she waited by the corral gate. She considered walking up to the men and politely asking about her session, and then anger triumphed. "If it's not too much trouble," she called, "would you mind getting a horse for me? I *did* make an appointment for a ride."

There was a moment of suspended action and then both men moved toward her, looking strangely alike in their worn jeans and long-sleeved flannel shirts. The slim one said something to his companion that made him laugh as they strolled along. Lucie noticed that the man with the stockier frame was gray-haired, but the tall, lean employee who moved easily beside him was in his early thirties. He had thick, straw-colored hair that had been bleached by the sun until it looked almost colorless against his tanned skin. Lucie returned his calm gray-eyed glance with one of her own which was just as assessing. If he was the man who would accompany her on the ride, he didn't appear enchanted by the prospect. That was all right—neither was she.

"I'm sorry, miss," the older man said as they came up to her. "I didn't know you wanted anything special—thought you just came down to look over the stock. Did you say something about an appointment?"

"I certainly did. My name's on the list in there," she said, nodding toward the hut. "Lucinda Forsythe. I phoned before lunch."

He frowned and scratched his head. "Nobody said anything to me. The trouble is—whoever's walking by answers the danged phone if I'm not around. I'm afraid the afternoon trail riders left a half hour ago. You'll have to wait till morning or go out on your own."

Lucie's eyes widened as she glanced toward the corral's occupants. "But I've never been here before and I don't know much about horses." Which was an understatement if there ever was one, she thought angrily.

"Then you'd do better to wait til morning," the corral manager announced. "We have a beginner's group that leaves at nine. I'll put your name down for it."

"My name is already down for this afternoon," she reminded him in a way that made him straighten with surprise. "Tomorrow is too late. Surely there must be someone who can take me out." She let her steady gaze rest on the younger man.

"There's nobody fitting except me," the older man argued, only to have his sidekick interrupt, with a gesture.

"I can work it in, Jed," he said, speaking for the first time. "If it's okay with you—and Miss . . ." He paused, presumably having forgotten her name.

"Forsythe," she snapped.

He nodded and leveled his broad-brimmed hat to shade his eyes. "Yes, ma'am," he said, unimpressed. "If you'll wait in the hut, Miss Forsythe, I'll saddle Marmaduke."

Lucie's eyebrows rose. "You'll saddle who?"

"Marmaduke—over there." He jerked his head toward the trough. "The black one. Is that right, Jed?"

The older man nodded slowly. "If that's what Miss Forsythe wants, I'll get a saddle." When there was no response, he moved off down to a section of fence where four saddles rested on the top rail.

His companion started to follow when Lucie caught at his sleeve. She shot an anxious glance toward the corral as she said tersely, "That one called Marmaduke—he's awfully big."

"We don't grow stunted ones, ma'am."

He appeared to tack the last word on deliberately and Lucie narrowed her eyes to give him a suspicious look. There was no getting around it; the man was almost a prototype for the cowboy she'd seen in magazine ads. Broad shoulders, slim hips, and wrinkles at the corners of his eyes that came from squinting at the sun. He reminded her of all the clichés—roundups, little dogies, and evenings around a campfire. Undoubtedly he could strum a guitar and possibly furnish an effective baritone to accompany the music. Another swift glance and she altered her thinking about that. With his rugged profile, he wouldn't have to sing for his supper to satisfy the lodge's feminine guests. All he had to do was lean on the fence and wave as the tour buses rolled in.

"Was there anything else, ma'am?"

She came back to earth in a hurry as his dry comment penetrated, and then colored under his surveillance.

"Not if you can ride a horse," she flared.

He took his time about answering. "I can manage. I thought *you* were the one we were worrying about." When she would have interrupted, he went on blandly, "Duke's been around a while but his manners are good. I can get him ready in no time. There's coffee in the hut if you'd like to wait in there."

His thinly veiled amusement triggered Lucie's temper. "I've already waited longer than I planned—oh, never mind." She brushed back a strand of hair from her flushed cheek. "I'll go stand in the shade."

"You do that, ma'am." His voice sharpened, abandoning the classic drawl to say, "And find a hat someplace. You'll need it for the ride."

"I'll be perfectly all right without one."

He ignored her protest completely. "There's a brimmed straw in the hut. I think some kid left it behind—but it'll serve."

"I said that it won't be necessary. At this rate, the sun will be down before we get started." She turned and walked toward the shady spot under the eaves of the hut, hoping the temperature was lower out of the glare.

The older man passed her on the way, carrying a saddle and bridle. "Won't be long now, miss," he assured her.

"Fine. Oh, just a minute," she said, stopping him when he would have moved on. "The man who's going with me—I'd better know his name."

"Sure. It's Max. He's a good rider, so you won't have to worry. Besides, ol' Duke only has one gait. Dead slow. Unless it's dinner time," he added, shoulders shaking at his own humor. "Then don't get in the way of the feed trough."

"It looks to me as if he hasn't bothered to move away from it most of his life," Lucie said, frowning as she saw how Max had to yank on the horse's rope bridle to get him beyond reach of a straw pile. "Has Duke always weighed so much?"

"Off and on. But the old boy doesn't have a mean bone in his body—that's the important thing for you. If you want to borrow a hat, there's one on the back of the door." He jerked his head toward the hut. "Just bring it back when you're through."

"I've already told Max that it isn't necessary."

Jed frowned. "At this altitude, you can get burned even when there's a cloud cover."

"Thanks, but I'll be all right," Lucie said, wishing to heaven that she'd never bothered with the damned ride in the first place. When she visited her mother and stepfather, she'd just ignore the outdoor activities at McLaren's resort. Unfortunately, it was too late for such a maneuver now.

"Whatever you say, miss." Jed gave up without any more convincing and went on to the corral.

By then, it wasn't worth the effort of walking to the hut, so Lucie moved across and leaned against a nearby ponderosa pine, relaxing in its shade.

It was peaceful there. Other than the fluid movements of the two men as they set about persuading the big black horse that he had work to do, there was little to disturb the sunny afternoon. Occasionally she could hear noise from the highway at the boundary of the resort grounds because the arterial to Yellowstone National Park to the north was a busy one. The resort where she was staying at Jackson Lake attracted visitors who liked more luxury with their natural wonders. Instead of traveling with campers or backpacks, guests viewed the majestic Tetons from a free-form swimming pool or from the balconies of their snug cottages. There were carefully designed nature trails for the more venturesome and tennis courts for guests who preferred the familiar.

Lucie had passed a barbeque pit en route to the corral and wasn't surprised to find there were unobtrusive awnings which could be unfurled in case of rain or "cloud cover," as Jed put it.

She found herself wishing that more clouds would gather overhead at that moment instead of scudding across the intensely blue sky. She brushed at a fly who had gotten sidetracked on his way to the barbecue and watched him buzz away, looking for new fields to conquer. A covert glance at the corral showed that Max was busy slipping the bit in Duke's mouth before reaching up to settle the bridle on the horse's head. Lucie watched through narrowed eyes and rubbed the end of her nose absently. A fleeting memory made her frown. What was that old proverb about noses that itched? It was some ridiculous story about kissing a fool. There was another about snakes being found near pools where horses drink.

She remembered that one when she saw Max swing easily onto a big gray mount by the water trough and take Duke's reins from Jed. He waited for the older man to open the railed gate and then brought both horses up to the path alongside the fence.

Lucie went to meet the procession, trying to hide her reluctance.

Max was about to hand her the black horse's reins when some of her uncertainty must have gotten through to him. He dismounted and, leading both horses to a concrete step arrangement on the path, said, "Come over here. It's easier than giving you a leg up." By then, he'd tossed the gray's reins over the fence rail and the horse waited obediently.

Marmaduke's manners weren't as commendable. The big horse snorted and whisked his tail as he watched Lucie's wary approach. When she got alongside, he jerked his head up and snuffled noisily. At least, "snuffled" was the polite word for it. Actually, it was a violent, gutsy horse laugh, and when Lucie shot a furious look at him, she noticed the remnants of a grin on Max's face.

He wiped it off before she could comment. "Duke

veers to the lazy side. You'll have to be firm," he said, tugging the horse closer to the steps so she could mount. "I'll fix those stirrups once you get aboard. They're a little long."

Lucie managed to mount without trouble but gasped when Duke immediately started moving off.

"Pull him up," Max commanded, making a belated grab for the bridle. "For pete's sake, show him who's boss."

Lucie swallowed, trying not to show she was already suffering from altitude sickness. It was like being on a second-floor windowsill—only windowsills didn't jolt around.

"Put your feet in the stirrups, will you?" Max told her impatiently, giving another jerk to the bridle when Duke edged toward the straw pile. "Otherwise, we'll never get out of the damned corral."

Lucie had an overpowering urge to say that was all right with her. Her resolve to become a proficient horsewoman had evaporated the minute she'd touched the saddle. It wasn't bad enough that she had no control over the horse beneath her; his back was so broad that she could barely get her feet in the stirrups.

Apparently the stirrups were only going to be part of her trouble. Max looked at her shoes as he was shortening the leather straps and said, "You'll have a devil of a time riding this horse in a pair of loafers. I hope you can keep them on."

Lucie was more worried about keeping herself on. "Don't worry. I can manage," she told him and clutched the reins, thankful that she'd seen enough Western movies to know how to do that.

Max got back on his own horse and led the way down the path. Lucie's mount trailed along reluctantly after Max delivered a forceful slap on his rump.

Lucie resisted an impulse to clutch the saddle horn as Marmaduke moved along the rocky path which dipped across a dry ravine before starting up the hill behind the corral. It didn't take more than fifteen feet of the horse's lurching over the rock-strewn path before she called to the man riding ahead of her. "Exactly how long will this ride take?" Then, before he could turn in the saddle to answer her, she went on hurriedly, "I don't want to inconvenience you. Just a short tour will do fine."

Max spoke over his shoulder. "Nobody wants to shortchange you, Miss Forsythe. You'll get the regular trip that you paid for. Incidentally, I'd better introduce myself—since we're going to be together an hour or so . . ."

"An hour or so!" Her horrified exclamation cut him off. "I was thinking in terms of a *half* hour. Actually I have a date," she tacked on, since that sounded like a valid reason for cutting things short. "And I know your name, Max—the other man told me."

"Jed did?"

"Yes, of course. If there was any trouble, I didn't want to have to say, 'Hey you!' "

"I see." He settled his hat more firmly, shading his expression. "You won't be in any trouble if you keep Duke's head up. Don't let him browse along the trail like that!" he added sharply. "Yank on the reins."

"I'm yanking," she panted.

"Use some muscle, for God's sake," he went on as Duke reached for another clump of grass.

"I don't want to hurt him."

"You won't—not the way you're going. That's better. Now—nudge him in the ribs or we'll be out here for the night."

"What do I—nudge him—with?" Lucie asked, feeling perspiration run down her back. She flexed her fingers, which already were cramped from clutching the reins.

Max pulled up again. "You nudge him with your heels, Miss Forsythe," he started in a painfully polite tone. Then, when there was a thud on the path, he added, "Sit still. I'll pick up your shoe. Keep that horse's head up!"

"You don't have to shout—"

"Sorry." He swung to the ground, holding his reins in one hand as he picked up her loafer and shoved it back on her foot. Then he put both the foot and the loafer vigorously back in the stirrup. "You'd better use the quirt—that rawhide piece on the back of the saddle," he went on, frowning up at her. "Whap him on the rear with it when he starts dragging his feet." Max got back on his horse then and watched her attempt to follow his instructions. "Not that way—you're not supposed to stroke him to sleep. Make it sting, Miss Forsythe. Never mind—you lead the way and I'll bring up the rear. That way I can keep the lazy bas—" Max broke off and finished lamely, "keep Duke going."

Lucie drew a breath of relief. "That's fine with me. Except I don't know which way to go."

"There's only one path. Try to stay on it."

"I'll do my level best," she told him through clenched teeth, wishing she could use the quirt on him instead of the horse. "Be sure and tell me when it's time to start back."

"Believe me," he assured her, "I won't forget."

From then on, she continued to ride with her teeth clenched. For one thing, it fitted her mood and for another, she found it didn't hurt so much when Marmaduke lurched along. Each time he took a step, Lucie could feel her vertebrae crunch and, unless she kept her jaw firm, her teeth jar, as well.

Of course it was ridiculous to dwell on her aches and pains, but at the moment, there wasn't much else in view. The scenery consisted mainly of Marmaduke's dusty neck and his ears, which were flattened back most of the time, showing that he wasn't in any better mood than his rider.

Lucie tried to concentrate on the grassy hillside with its scattered pine trees or the blue sky overhead, but her mount seemed to sense when her attention wandered and he immediately reached for anything edible at the trailside. This automatically brought forth a terse "Keep his head up," from the man in back of her. There were variations, ranging from "Use your reins," to "Kick him in the ribs," and finally "For God's sake, woman—make him *move.*" By the last command, Lucie was ready for a nervous breakdown—as well as aching in every bone.

A moment later, they reached the top of the hill and the path widened enough for Max to bring his mount alongside. "Most people stop here and admire the view," he said. "Pull up your horse."

Lucie's jaw dropped. "Well, I must say, that's certainly a switch," she muttered, yanking on the reins. "Whoa, Duke—" Her voice rose unhappily. It seemed that Marmaduke didn't like *that* order either.

Max didn't bother with words. He simply leaned across his saddle and caught hold of the black horse's bridle, dragging him to a standstill. Then he turned to Lucie. "If you'd like to get down for a few minutes, this is your chance."

She considered the offer and shook her head. "If I got down," she said truthfully, "I'd never make it back up again, and it's a long way to the corral. That's the lodge over there, isn't it?"

Max nodded. "And Jackson Lake beyond by the Tetons." He gestured down toward the bottom of the hill. "There's a beaver dam on that little lake over to the left. See it—just past that pair of swans."

Lucie was able to relax and follow his gaze since he seemed to have Duke under control, giving her the chance to ease one foot out of the stirrup and flex some muscles that she feared atrophied forever. "It's really beautiful country," she admitted, wishing they could have talked like ordinary human beings earlier. It had been a bad beginning, and then riding single file along that miserable narrow trail didn't help. Lucie hadn't dared sneak any looks over her shoulder and she couldn't have been an inspiring figure, trying to remain upright in the saddle. She risked another glance at the man's firmly etched profile as he stared at the panorama in front of them, and decided to make a stab at improving relations. "This must be a nice place to work," she began tentatively. "Do you live around here?"

He turned to let his glance rake over her. "Not far away. In my line of work I have to travel quite a bit. The season's over here in a couple weeks."

"I'd forgotten about that," she said, color staining her cheeks under his scrutiny. "Where do you go then?"

"South. I've another place lined up in Arizona that'll carry me through the winter. How about you?"

"Me? Oh, I have a job in San Francisco."

"In a nice, steam-heated office?"

"With a sun lamp on weekends," she said, sounding defensive. "I like it that way."

"There's nothing wrong with it. I'm just surprised that you picked this place for your vacation. Maybe the lodge'll give you a refund if you complain."

"I'm not here on a tour," Lucie informed him, deciding he'd gotten his quota of entertainment out of her predicament. "It's family business."

"That should be pleasant."

"Not really." Her lips tightened. "I'm not looking forward to it at all. It's a case of 'duty calls.'"

"Sorry—I didn't mean to sound inquisitive."

"You couldn't know." To change the subject, she pointed toward some white blossoms blanketing the ground around them. "Those are pretty. What are they called?"

"Yarrow. It turns to a rust color when it goes to seed," he said, but refused to be sidetracked by the local plant life. "I take it you're traveling alone?"

"For the moment. I have to meet someone tomorrow." She checked her watch as she remembered her plans for later that afternoon. "I'd better be starting back." Her lips curved slightly. "I'm sure that won't break your heart. It was nice of you to come along. You must get awfully sick of nursing greenhorns day after day."

"It has its moments." Straightening in the saddle, he let go of Duke's bridle and the big black immediately shifted restlessly toward the sheer edge of the viewpoint. Lucie gasped and Max's arm shot out again, yanking Duke back to the path while he kept his own mount under control with his other hand.

The path had widened and started down before he eventually released Duke, urging him ahead.

Lucie turned to give Max a rueful grin as they passed, although her cheeks were still pale from the maneuver on the hilltop. "I thought I'd try skydiving sometime, but I really didn't plan to start today," she said.

"It would be better without the horse," he agreed.

Max didn't say any more, and when Duke would have lingered over a tasty morsel after that, he moved the gray horse along behind him like a bulldozer. That—together with some strange chirruping noises which Lucie couldn't translate but Duke evidently could—kept them moving.

As they wound down to within sight of the railed corral, Marmaduke finally shed his reluctance and set a pace that had her bouncing in the saddle. By then, it took real determination for her to keep from clutching the pommel for the last fifty yards. Certainly it wouldn't have affected Marmaduke's plans; he had his eye on the straw pile and would have endured the Charge of the Light Brigade to get there.

He pulled up with a flourish alongside the trough in the corral and stretched out his neck. Lucie was a little late dropping the reins so when Max drew alongside, he found her nose down in Duke's dusty mane—embracing his sweaty neck, virtually impaled on the saddle horn in the process.

She straightened painfully, keeping a stony expression as he swung off his horse and adjusted the reins so that they wouldn't drag. "I'll be with you in a minute," he said in a muffled voice over his shoulder. "Better let me help you down."

Lucie would have liked to tell him it wasn't necessary. She also would have liked to slip down out of the saddle easily, landing lightly on her feet. Then, after that, she would have given Duke's neck a careless pat and turned to bestow a casual, charming smile on Max before she walked gracefully up the path to the lodge.

What actually happened was that she remained slumped in the saddle, knowing that if she tried to dismount by herself, she'd spill onto the ground in an untidy heap by Duke's feet. At least if that happened, she wouldn't have to worry about being stepped on. From the way Duke's jaw was functioning, the black horse obviously had no intention of moving as long as the feed trough stayed where it was.

Lucie flexed her fingers to get some circulation stirring and then brushed the back of her hand over her hot face. She wished she had a chance to comb her hair and mop her cheeks, but Max had stored her clutch purse in his saddlebag at the beginning of the ride.

As he finally appeared around Duke's derriere, he solemnly handed the purse up to her. "Take your feet out of the stirrups," he instructed, putting his hands at her waist.

"I *know* that . . ." she began, and found herself still sputtering as he plucked her off the horse to bring her down in front of him.

It should have been a simple maneuver but somehow it didn't turn out that way because Max was standing close to Duke and the big horse didn't give way in the interchange. Lucie was brought down slowly between them. She felt her legs inch past the tall man's chest and then was made aware of his taut thigh muscles under his worn jeans. That was startling enough but when the upper part of her body was given the sandwich treatment against his hard chest, her face flared with color.

"I'm sorry about that," he muttered, stepping back after she was on the ground.

"Honestly!" Lucie said, drawing herself up indignantly and then spoiling the effect when her knees gave way and she had to clutch at his shirt front, pulling it open in the process. She tried to ignore the expanse of bronzed chest in front of her, knowing that to an onlooker it must seem as if she couldn't keep her hands off him. "I'm sorry. My knees won't work. If I could just—"

"Sit down?" he asked noncommitally.

"Oh, no!" At that moment, sitting down was not to

be considered. "Maybe I could lean against the fence for a minute."

"You'd be better off in the shade," he said, shoring her up against him and leading her to the gate. "Try leaning against the tree over there while I get you a cup of coffee from the hut." He stashed her against the pine trunk like a piece of lumber. "If you're not used to riding, it can take a while to get your circulation going again. Are you okay?"

"Fine," she said, knowing she wasn't convincing anybody.

The coffee helped—even though Max admitted as he gave it to her that she'd probably be better off with a glass of cold water.

"No—really, this is fine," Lucie insisted again. She wished she could linger and give her knees a chance to regain their stiffening, but she felt uneasy keeping him from his work. "You go right ahead if you have something you want to do," she told him awkwardly. "I imagine your boss keeps you busy," she added, trying to think of a safe topic as he stayed close, leaning against the fence rail near her.

"Keeping the customers happy is the most important part as far as Jed is concerned."

"Then it's strange he isn't here to do it," she said, frowning as she looked around the deserted grounds.

"He's probably down in the stable by now."

When Max, showing no inclination to join his employer, let the silence lengthen, Lucie gulped the rest of her coffee so fast that it was almost painful. Anything was better than standing there under his analytical masculine gaze.

She looked around when she finished, clutching the empty styrofoam cup. "Where do I leave this?"

"I'll take care of it later," Max said, reaching over and depositing it on the nearest fence post.

"Well then—" Lucie started to brush her palms and stopped in mid-stroke, realizing how silly she looked. She bent to retrieve her purse from the ground and almost groaned out loud as she straightened.

Max stayed stubbornly where he was, and it suddenly occurred to Lucie that he might expect a tip after escorting a trail rider. She rubbed her forehead fretfully as she tried to remember how much the damned ride had cost in the first place. Did cowboys get tipped fifteen percent or was that the horse? Maybe Duke expected him to pool the proceeds. The ridiculous possibilities crowded out everything else and she started to laugh.

Surprisingly enough, her amusement wasn't shared. "Something funny, Miss Forsythe?" Max asked, his eyebrows coming together in an ominous line.

"No. Not really." Lucie was tempted to mention her dilemma but his tone made her decide against it. The best thing to do, she concluded, was palm some currency and transfer it as she shook hands in farewell. Until then, she hadn't planned anything more than a simple good-by, but things were getting more complicated all the time.

She lowered her gaze and tried to extract the bills from her purse unobtrusively. While that was happening, she missed Max's considering expression and the way he shoved his hat to the back of his head as if he'd come to a decision.

"I wonder if you'd have dinner with me tonight, Miss Forsythe?"

"I beg your pardon?" She looked up, startled.

"I asked if you'd have dinner."

His grave tone almost mesmerized her, but she remembered just in time. "I'm sorry. I already have a dinner date."

"Could it be broken?"

For an instant, she was tempted to capitulate. Then she shook her head, as much to get her thoughts under control as in reply. What in the dickens was she hesitating about? If she couldn't manage a conversation with the man over one cup of coffee, a dinner date would be catastrophic. She didn't even dare meet his glance or he'd see how aware she was of his physical magnetism. Which was ridiculous when she considered it.

She came back to the present in a hurry as she heard him drawl, "Did Duke damage your vocal equipment, too?"

"That's about the only thing still in mint condition. I'm sorry about dinner, but I do have another date. And the way I'm feeling now," she confessed with a rueful smile, "I should have scheduled a visit to the masseuse instead." She extended her hand. "Thank you, Max. I'm sure you did your best. It's too bad that I don't have any talent."

Automatically his hand came out to grasp hers. "It just takes time and practice," he said, and then broke off as he felt the currency pressed in his palm. "What's this?"

To her chagrin, he examined the bills quite deliberately and reached out for her purse to put them back inside. "I never take money for tips, Miss Forsythe. It's against my principles," he told her solemnly. "Now if you want to really show your appreciation . . ."

Lucie was so confused by then that she didn't resist when his strong hands came up to grasp her shoulders and pull her tight against him, letting her feel the disturbing warmth of his body. Panic struck her when his mouth was just a whisper away and her lips parted in protest.

At that instant, another masculine voice shattered the scene. "Mac—you son of a gun! That must have been some ride! I thought you hadn't even met the girl, or is that just a brotherly kiss?"

The man holding her straightened without losing any of his dignity, but Lucie heard cold withdrawal in his voice as he said, "Better look again, Vito. Lucinda just had some dirt in her eye." He pretended to scan her bewildered face and then shook his head. "Damned if I can see anything. If it continues to bother you, you'd better check with the nurse up at the hotel. Vito can probably take you up there now." He turned to the other man. "Why don't you go in and call from the hut first? See if the medical office is open." He exerted enough pressure on Lucie's wrist as he spoke to keep her from protesting.

They both watched Vito nod hurriedly and say, "Sure, I'll check right away. Be back in a minute," before he turned and made for the hut.

He had barely disappeared inside when Lucie recovered her voice. "What in the dickens is going on? There's nothing wrong with my eye—and what did he mean about meeting me and a brotherly kiss?" Her voice broke on the last word as the full import sank in. "Oh, Lord," she breathed. "Don't tell me that . . ."

The man beside her simply nodded, his expression so grim that he might have been surveying a disaster area rather than welcoming a new member of the family.

"You're Andrew McLaren?" Lucie persisted, as if hoping for a final reprieve.

"Guilty as charged, I'm afraid." He cast an impatient glance toward the doorway of the hut. "I'll explain it later. When we have a few minutes alone."

"It seems to me you've had more than enough time already, Mr. McLaren." Lucie's voice matched his cool formality. "I'm going back to my cottage now. You can make up whatever story you want to tell Vito—since you seem to be so good at concocting fiction."

He murmured something incomprehensible as she turned. "I beg your pardon," she said, looking back at him.

"Never mind," he said grimly. "I'd better start mending family fences at this point instead of tearing them down."

"You can try, Mr. McLaren. You can always try," she told him politely and walked away.

Chapter

-2-

It was an hour later when she heard a knock on the door of her cottage. She took her time in answering, giving a cursory glance around the bedroom on the way to the door. The pleasant teak furnishings went well with the royal blue bedspread, and the blue and white chintz covering on the upholstered chairs was beyond reproach. Lucie took another two seconds to check her own appearance in a full-length mirror and nodded thoughtfully. It would have been hard to find a greater contrast to her dusty jeans and shirt of the afternoon than the green silk trouser outfit with its snug-fitting top. The bodice design featured a deep V-neckline which counteracted any demure effect that the long sleeves might have had, and there were matching high-heeled sandals to complete the picture. Whatever that picture might be, it was hardly the reflection of a sister or the girl next door.

Which was just what she intended, Lucie thought bitterly, not having forgotten the events of the afternoon.

Another knock sounded, in more demanding fashion this time. A small smile lightened Lucie's expression as she reached for the knob and pulled the door open without haste. She surveyed Drew McLaren's figure waiting on the porch and let her eyebrows go up in assumed surprise. "Oh, it's you," she said, stepping out to peer past him. "I was expecting Vito."

"Vito," he replied, drawling the word out into two distinct syllables, "relinquished some of his time to me. I told him that we'd join him in the lobby a little later." He held the door and motioned her back into the cottage. "I thought there were a few things we should set straight."

Lucie frowned and glanced around at the gathering dusk on the resort grounds. Already lights were turned on in the big lodge, barely visible beyond the clumps of trees which kept the cottages in pleasant isolation from the main building. There were only winding gravel roads to connect them, and it was necessary for guests to use the primitive tracks if they chose to take their meals at the lodge.

"It's getting dark," Lucie said, lingering on the porch. "Why don't we postpone this conference until another time?"

"If you're thinking of those high heels," he said, taking in her outfit with a comprehensive glance, "don't worry. The management furnishes a flashlight with every cottage and I'll light the way with it to make sure that you don't twist an ankle when we go for dinner." He watched her move carefully back into the cottage after his assurance and went on with an undertone of laughter, "You have enough to think about without a sprained ankle, as well."

Lucie's lips thinned in exasperation. She might have known. Even after she'd soaked in a hot tub until she practically shriveled, he'd immediately noted that she was still suffering from that damned horseback ride. She took a deep breath and went over to ease onto the arm of a chair. "At least I don't have a guilty conscience. Aren't you a little old for playing games and using an assumed name?"

He abandoned his restless tour around the room and settled in another chair to survey her dispassionately. "I didn't give you the wrong name," he said. "You just weren't listening closely. Jed, down at the corral, calls me Mac. That's what happens with a last name like mine. Most acquaintances call me Andrew or Mac. Only my relatives and close friends call me Drew."

She gave him a disapproving glance. "That still doesn't excuse you. You knew what you were doing all along and I can't see what you hoped to gain by it. Unless you thought you'd catch me in some awful gaffe before I tumbled to your identity."

"That's ridiculous. Why would I want to do a thing like that?"

His voice was matter-of-fact, but Lucie still surveyed him suspiciously. She had to acknowledge that he didn't look as if he had any untoward ideas. Despite his well-fitting coffee-colored suede blazer and beige wool slacks, he looked like the same assured individual she'd met earlier in the day.

Lucie found herself coloring slightly under his level look and replied to his question with the first thing that came into her head. "I felt that you might not be happy about your father marrying again." When he frowned, she plunged on, "Well, you didn't come to the wedding, so what else could I think?"

"That possibly there was a reason why I couldn't attend the ceremony," he said drily. "Since my father and your mother didn't seem unduly upset, I don't see why you're up in arms. Incidentally, I phoned them in Hawaii earlier today and they sent their love to you."

"They're both all right?"

"They certainly sounded like it." A fleeting grin crossed his tanned face. "And I think they're old enough to take care of themselves on a honeymoon without our help." He leaned back in the chair and crossed his long legs. "Incidentally, they'd like to find you down home when they get back."

She stared at him, uncomprehending. "You mean at your resort in Arizona?"

"Of course. That's home base. You can stay in the family quarters or in the lodge—whichever you prefer."

"I'm sorry, but it isn't possible this trip," she said hastily. "I can't spare the time. I explained to your father before they left. There was hardly enough time for me to detour by here now, but they wanted . . ."

". . . us to get together?"

Lucie wasn't sure that she liked Drew's lifted eyebrows or the tone of his voice. "They seemed to feel it was important," she replied.

"But you weren't crazy about the idea?"

There was no mistaking the way his thoughts were going and Lucie saw no point in evading the issue. "That's right. I'd managed without a brother for twenty-three years and there was a good chance that we'd get together over the Christmas holidays, so I didn't see the need of my making a special trip to Wyoming now. *Especially* since you hadn't made any special efforts to get to California and the wedding." When he started to protest, she went on unheedingly. "And from the way you acted this afternoon, I don't think you were exactly thrilled to welcome me into the family circle."

"Have you finished?"

The words came out in an even tone, but there was something about it that made Lucie bite her lip and murmur, "I'm sorry if I've offended you. But you did make me feel like an awful fool on that miserable horse and afterward when you . . . you . . ."

"Discovered something in your eye?"

Lucie reddened but met his gaze defiantly. "It was fun and games all the way for you, wasn't it? I think I have a right to be annoyed."

"You weren't too unhappy at the time," he pointed out. "Other than some aches and pains from your session with Duke, and I wasn't responsible for that."

"You know I didn't mean that," she countered. "What excuse did you give Vito when he finished phoning?"

Drew folded his arms over his chest. "Ah, yes—Vito Perelli. I wondered when we'd get around to him. How did you manage a dinner date in such short order? He said you'd just met this afternoon."

"What's wrong with having—" She broke off and scowled. "That's none of your affair. You still haven't told me what happened after I left."

"Practically nothing. There wasn't any medical appointment to cancel because the nurse was off-duty this afternoon. It was a safe enough dodge to get Vito out of the way for a few minutes. When he came back, I just said that your eye was much better and that you'd gone ahead to change clothes." Drew paused to shift in his chair. "I also said that we'd be a threesome for dinner. Since he knew that I was planning to join you here, it would be damned strange if we didn't at least eat dinner together. You can add him to your social schedule later on if he's worth it."

"You're certainly caustic about your friends."

"Vito Perelli is just an acquaintance who's stayed at our resort several times. I ran into him here earlier today."

Lucie decided that comment was as much as Drew would unbend regarding the other man. Since she was going to be around such a short time, a threesome for dinner was probably the best arrangement. Vito Perelli could be hard to discourage on his own, and Drew certainly didn't fall in the bland "older brother" category she'd allotted him.

"Your plans for dinner sound fine," she said aloud. "Vito just introduced himself down by the corral this afternoon and when he suggested getting together later, it was better than eating alone." A glimmer of a smile lightened her expression. "At that point, I didn't know you were on the premises."

"It's a good thing that Vito didn't hear that. He fancies himself as a ladies man, and coming in one step above a vacant place at the table wouldn't do much for his ego."

"From what I saw, his ego is in no danger of top-pling." Lucie leaned on the back of the chair, wincing as she moved. "What does Mr. Perelli do for a living?"

"Importing and selling, I guess. From the way he talks, he gets around. He came over to talk to me in the lobby when I registered. Since he's stayed at our place, we have some mutual acquaintances."

Lucie nodded thoughtfully. Although she'd never been a guest at McLaren's resort near the south rim of the Grand Canyon in Arizona, some of her acquaintances had and rated it as a topflight guest lodge. For an instant, she wished that she hadn't been so adamant in her refusal to greet the newlyweds there on their return. But if she began as she meant to go on, Drew McLaren wouldn't be able to accuse her of battening on to his family's bank account.

She had just reached that laudable conclusion when she noticed that Drew had leaned forward and was snapping his fingers to bring her out of her brown study.

"Back with it again?" he asked when she straightened self-consciously. "I don't know whether it's my company or jet fatigue that's bothering you, but whatever it is—"

"Probably it's all that fresh air this afternoon." She managed to get to her feet. "Some food should help. If Vito isn't waiting in the lobby, maybe I can sneak a cup of coffee and wake up." She went over to her opened suitcase on a luggage rack against the wall and unpacked a long mink scarf. It was a designer piece of rich brown, and Lucie saw Drew eyeing it as he helped put it around her shoulders.

"A fringe benefit from work," she explained, making things clear. "My employers are nice about markdowns."

"You mean I can expect chinchilla and sable in the near future?" he asked, looking amused.

"Not unless I find them on a clearance table." She shivered slightly as she opened the door of the cottage and a determined breeze made itself felt. "I hope it's warmer than this when I get farther south."

He came to join her, securing the door behind them. "The Chamber of Commerce will do its best, but don't pack away that fur scarf. Nights can be cold in our part of the country."

"I'll remember. It's good that you thought to bring the flashlight. I didn't realize it would get dark so fast."

"We're close to the end of the season here. They've already had the first snowfall up the road at Yellowstone," Drew commented, switching on the beam as they reached the graveled surface which served as both road and sidewalk up to the lodge.

On either side of them thick clumps of shrubbery were interspersed between shade trees to provide privacy for the guests in the cottages. During the day, Lucie had enjoyed the feeling of isolation, but suddenly she realized that she would welcome the bright lights of the lodge when they arrived.

Drew's hand was cupped protectively around her elbow as they strolled along and he must have felt her shiver. "Cold?" he asked.

"No." She shook her head and then realized it was a wasted motion in the dark. "Someone's walking over my grave. That's what comes from living in cities. I'll probably never get to sleep tonight for the quiet. That's certainly 'a wide and starry sky'—" She broke off abruptly when her shoe slipped in the gravel.

"Watch where you're going," he instructed, tightening his grip. "There's no need to follow Mr. Stevenson's dictates so faithfully."

Her steps slowed. "What do you mean?"

"Well, the next line in that poem goes 'dig the grave and let me lie.' If that's what an afternoon on horseback does, you'd better take up croquet."

She started to laugh. "I may ache in every bone but I'm not desperate yet. And the one thing that's undamaged is my appetite. I feel as hungry as Duke did this afternoon. Probably it's fresh air that makes him so ravenous—" Her voice dropped as another sound cut through the nighttime stillness. "Is that a car coming?"

They both glanced behind them automatically.

"I don't see any lights," Drew started to say when suddenly his fingers bit painfully into her arm. "My God—that fool's crazy! There isn't room to get around us—"

That was all Lucie heard him say. The next instant she was flying through the air to land sprawled over a shrub at the edge of the track—as a car blazed past on the road where they'd been standing.

Chapter

−3−

Lucie wasn't sure how much time passed before she became aware that the shrub had hundreds of sharp twigs and every one of them was poked painfully into her. She groaned and struggled to get upright. At the same moment she heard movement nearby and then a sentence or two of profanity that was remarkable for its precise pithy descriptions.

She tried to peer through the darkness. "Drew? Where are you?"

"Over here, Lucie—are you all right? Stay where you are until I can get to you."

By then, she was coherent enough to recognize the undertone of pain in his voice. It was with difficulty that she finally located the flickering flashlight on the ground fifteen feet to her left and moved stiffly over to pick it up. She flashed the light around and saw Drew's dark bulk as he tried to lever himself upright against a pine tree trunk. Her own aches and pains were forgotten as she darted toward him. "Drew, what's the matter? Where does it hurt?"

It was such a ridiculous question that he let out a bark of laughter which broke off as she touched him.

"Oh, God!" She drew back her hand. "How bad is it?"

"The damn car caught my thigh when I was trying to get out of the way. How about you?"

"I'm okay. My clothes got the worst of it. Can you stay there until I get help? You'll be better off on the ground if you start to pass out," she told him as he struggled to his feet.

"I am now *off* the ground and I have no intention of passing out," he told her in a tone that defied argument. "Let me lean on you and I can make it."

"Not to the lodge—that's too far. We'd better go back to the cottage. I'll phone for help from there, if you think—oh!" She drew a startled breath as his groping hand covered the soft curve of her breast.

"Sorry." His fingers moved across to her arm. "Shake that flashlight and see if you can get it to work better."

"All right." She would liked to have borrowed a tree trunk just then and beaten her head against it. She was all kinds of a fool to let out that startled gasp when Drew's hand touched her in such an intimate way. If he'd needed any proof that her sophistication was just skin-deep, she'd certainly provided it.

"What's the matter?" Drew said in her ear. "Is something wrong with it?"

"Certainly not. I mean—what are you talking about?"

"The flashlight. What in the devil do you think?"

For the first time, Lucie blessed the dark for hiding her crimson cheeks. "The beam's pretty weak," she said, trying to sound brisk. "I think something *is* wrong with it."

"That's no surprise." His tone was dry as he reached out to take it from her. "We'll need it to get back to the cottage. Come around to my other side. If I can borrow your shoulder, I'll be okay."

"Is it your right leg that's hurt?"

"Go to the head of the class." The words were grated out as they moved slowly to the track and turned back toward the cottage. "Damned fool of a driver. He didn't even hesitate. Probably drunk as a coot."

"I hope that he's in a deep ditch someplace by now," Lucie said uncharitably. "You'd have thought he was aiming for us. Probably you shouldn't even be walking till you know what's wrong. Lord knows what you're doing to yourself." She peered anxiously at his tall figure hobbling along beside her.

"Stop fussing. If I'd stayed flat on the ground, I'd end up with pneumonia." Drew sounded very much like an irritable member of the family. "And there's no use calling the lodge for assistance. The only thing on duty tonight is a first aid box."

Lucie drew up, appalled. "You certainly need more than that."

"I know." He urged her on again. "The closest help is probably the hospital in Jackson. They'll have somebody on emergency duty."

Lucie nodded, happy to see the outlines of her cottage in the feeble illumination of the flashlight. She found her key and unlocked the door, reaching inside to snap on the bedroom light before helping Drew across the threshold. A quick look upward at his gray, drawn face made her lead him straight to the big bed in the center of the room. "Lie down. I'll do the telephoning."

He stubbornly propped himself against the headboard as he settled on the edge of the mattress. "The only person you have to call is Jed. He's on duty at the transportation desk. I left my car down at the corral earlier today. Ask him to get somebody to bring it here."

"All right," she agreed, turning to the phone. "But you're not driving anywhere—so don't get any ideas."

Drew stared at her, obviously puzzled, as she picked up the receiver and asked to be put through to the transporation desk as he'd instructed. Once she'd relayed the message and learned that the car could be delivered to the cottage within fifteen minutes, she hung up and turned back to face him. "So far, so good," she reported. "I'd better get into some other clothes or they'll think I'm the patient when we get to Jackson."

"Hold on," he said, before she'd taken more than a step toward the closet. "You don't have to drive into Jackson with me. Go ahead and keep your dinner date." He noted her suddenly stricken look. "Don't tell me you've forgotten Vito Perelli already."

"Oh, heavens." She put a hand to her cheek. "I wonder if he's still patiently waiting in the lobby."

A ring of the telephone cut into her words.

"Maybe he's in the lobby," Drew commented, "but he isn't patient."

Lucie waved him silent as she picked up the receiver. Vito let her know immediately that he was unhappy to learn she was still in the cottage instead of walking through the door of the lodge. Lucie bit her lip and tried to explain. "I was just going to have you paged, Mr. Perelli." There was another very short pause before she went on, "All right—Vito then. I'm sorry but I won't be able to make dinner tonight. I don't know whether it was the horseback ride or whether I'm coming down with something—but I feel grim. I hope you'll forgive me."

Vito's voice could be heard as she moved the receiver away from her ear to extract a shrubbery twig that she'd just discovered in her hair. "How is Drew?" she repeated a moment later. She looked over to the tall man stretched out atop her bed and watched him shake his head. "Fine, I guess. Didn't you get his message?" she said artlessly into the telephone mouthpiece. "He called me earlier and said that he'd have to postpone dinner with us. Something about a business appointment in town or somewhere—he wasn't explicit." She let her voice drop to a suggestive tone. "I really think it was with a woman and he didn't want to admit it. Having a member of the family around must cramp his style. "

There was a muttered comment from the bed to show what Drew thought of that, but Lucie ignored him as she gathered steam in her narrative. "Don't worry—I intend to ask him all sorts of questions in the morning." She waited patiently through Vito's answer. "I feel badly about tonight, too," she said finally, "but we'd better wait and see how tomorrow goes. Probably we'll run into each other in the lodge sometime during the morning—I'm sure I'll feel better by then. That's sweet of you. Good night, Vito."

"The man's persistent—if nothing else," Drew said, when she hung up and started for the closet again. "And I enjoyed the story. You'll have to tell me how it ends. What do you do—write fiction in your spare time?"

Lucie had the grace to look slightly ashamed. "Well, I couldn't tell him the truth . . ."

"You mean about the accident?"

"That too, but I really mean about ignoring our date. He might suspect my motives now, but that's better than learning that I'd forgotten all about him." She paused in the middle of pulling a skirt from a hanger. "And you didn't want me to go into any other details, did you?"

"Well, you could hardly tell the man that I was stretched out on your bed at the moment. On the other hand, you didn't have to intimate that I was on the tiles with a streetwalker."

She looked amused. "What difference does it make? Tomorrow, I can tell him you spent your evening at the library or calling on the mayor if it makes you feel better."

"Tomorrow, I'll make my own excuses, thanks."

"I still think you're upset over nothing." She paused at the door of the bathroom, carrying a sweater and skirt over one arm and holding a pair of low-heeled shoes in her hand. "From what I've seen of Mr. Perelli, he's the type who'll ask you if she has a friend."

"Yet you were going out with him."

"Only as far as the lodge dining room," she reminded.

"Then why the devil did you cancel it?" Drew asked, wincing slightly as he shifted on the mattress. "Jed could have gotten somebody to drive me into Jackson tonight."

"You're perfectly safe with me," Lucie announced coolly. "I thought that your father might prefer it this way. There are no strings attached."

"Oh, God, I'm sorry." Drew raked an impatient hand through his already tousled hair, leaving it standing on end. "I don't mean to sound like such a bastard—" He broke off again, realizing that he wasn't improving things. "I appreciate your efforts," he got out finally. "It's nice of you to go to so much trouble."

"Don't start polishing my halo. Vito Perelli isn't really my type," she replied, opening the bathroom door. "In the meantime, I'll get changed. The car should be here any minute."

Lucie had just finished changing when a horn sounded in front of the cottage. She emerged from the bathroom and pulled on a camel car coat before going over to peer out the window. "Do you own a black two-door something or other?"

"Well, it has two doors," Drew admitted, "and Jed's reliable, so it must be mine."

Lucie nodded and came back to the bedside. "Hang onto me. Is your leg worse?"

"I don't think so. It hurts like the devil, but I'm hoping it's just a bruised muscle."

"Are you going to be warm enough in that sports jacket?"

"There's a heater in the car. Besides, I don't want to go through the lodge. My room's on the third floor and Lord knows who I'd meet on the way."

"I could go for you," she offered tentatively.

"After telling Vito that you were *hors de combat?*" Drew shook his head and hobbled toward the door, keeping a hand on her shoulder. "Forget it. I'm just fine."

That was a blatant lie but Lucie knew better than to argue with him. Fortunately, his car turned out to be standard size rather than a compact, so he was able to sit in tolerable comfort. Drew waved aside her tentative suggestion that he'd be more comfortable in the back with his leg resting on the seat. Lucie started the car, vividly aware of his vibrant masculine presence in the confined space. Fortunately, her driving reflexes were automatic and she turned onto the road toward the main highway without revealing her feelings. When they passed the corral, she even managed to say, "I wonder if Marmaduke's conscience is bothering him after giving me such a bad time this afternoon."

"Don't you believe it! The only thing that would make Duke suffer is a lean night at the feedbag. Even so, I've been dickering to add him to the McLaren string." Drew turned and put his arm along the back of the seat. "We have lots of guests who haven't spent much time in a saddle. Old Duke is reliable and his riders are still aboard after an hour."

"That's because he's too broad to fall off."

"Probably. What you need to do is repeat the treatment tomorrow."

Lucie took her attention from the road long enough to bestow a look which, even in the half-light of the dashboard, showed what she thought of that suggestion.

"I mean it," he persisted. "The 'hair of the dog' treatment works."

Lucie slowed to turn onto the main road south to Jackson and then sent the speedometer up to the legal limit. "What makes you think so? The Inquisition wasn't any better the second time around. Besides, I have a perfect excuse—a plane reservation south in the afternoon. I made it before I was introduced to Duke."

"Also before you met me," Drew pointed out.

"Yes—well, I thought we'd meet in the morning and . . ." her voice trailed off uncertainly.

"Run out of things to say before noon?"

"Something like that. And I *do* have a reservation down to Phoenix. Of course, I didn't know you were going to be hurt," she added.

There was an uncomfortable silence then, which Drew made no effort to break. Instead, he stared straight ahead, and Lucie, from the corner of her eye, saw only his stern profile.

She turned her gaze back to the deserted highway which unwound like a ribbon under the car's headlights. At rare intervals, they'd meet a car speeding northward. Most of the campers and trailers which filled the highway during the day had evidently found a haven for the night. There were some scattered

guest ranches, proclaiming their presence with roadside signs near dirt turnoffs which led beyond the
foothills, but that was the only evidence of civilization.

Lucie finally couldn't endure the silence any longer.
"Are you all right?" she asked Drew in a taut tone.

He didn't respond immediately. It was almost as if
he had to think it over and she tensed, ready for the
bad news.

"About the same," he said, finally, and frowned as
the car made a sudden lurch before Lucie regained
control. "What the hell—!"

"I'm sorry," she cut in, not giving him time to finish. She couldn't very well admit that it was relief at
his reply which had made her attention lapse. For a
moment, she'd been afraid that pain had overcome
him. There wasn't any other logical excuse for his
withdrawal; he certainly couldn't have been upset by
the fact that she was leaving the next day. Perhaps
though, it would be better to soften her announcement. "Naturally, if the doctor has any discouraging
news," she said, trying to put it diplomatically, "I'll
stay as long as you need me. As soon as we find out,
I'll phone your father."

"No way."

"I beg your pardon?"

"I said," he replied definitely, "that there are to be
no long distance phone calls. I'm damned if my father's honeymoon is going to be spoiled."

"It's my mother's honeymoon, too," she flared back.
"Remember that."

"All the more reason. They're entitled to a few days
of peace without reports from us every hour."

Lucie squirmed uncomfortably behind the steering wheel. "Oh, all right. I didn't mean to give you a bad time, but you know very well that they'll be furious if they find out we've been hiding something."

"Well, why don't we wait and see what the doctor says. With any luck, he'll tell me to go back to the lodge, take a couple aspirin, and call him at ten in the morning."

Unfortunately, the treatment didn't turn out to be that simple. Once they arrived at the Jackson Hospital and Lucie helped him hobble into the emergency section, Drew insisted that she go find a cup of coffee instead of waiting around. Lucie agreed but only after making sure that he was settled and being looked after by an efficient-looking nurse while waiting for the doctor.

The same nurse brought him to the reception area of the hospital a half hour later in a wheelchair. Lucie's face must have mirrored her shock because Drew was quick to say, "Things aren't as bad as they look. The doctor just didn't want me wandering around the halls trying to find you."

"I should say not," the nurse put in indignantly. "He would have preferred that Mr. McLaren spend the night here in the hospital."

"But Mr. McLaren said 'no thanks,' " Drew replied firmly. "Lucie, would you mind driving up by the entrance so I can get out of this thing."

"Of course—if you're sure it's all right to leave," she began hesitantly.

"I'm sure. Very sure."

After that, it only took a few minutes before he was

transferred to the front seat of the car. Then, after thanking the nurse and repeating that he would indeed be careful, they were on the road back to the lodge.

"Would you like to have coffee or a sandwich before we get out of town?" Lucie asked, with an anxious look.

Drew shook his head. "They gave me some coffee while I was talking to the doctor. I think it was brewed last week. Maybe they were trying to drum up some new patients."

Lucie ignored that. "See here," she said severely, "aren't you ever going to tell me what they said?"

"Well—nothing's broken, thank God. It's mainly a bruise. Jogging's out for a day or so," he concluded flippantly.

"If you don't come through with details, you'll be back in that wheelchair," she warned, "—with a head injury this time."

"Okay, but watch the road, will you?" he complained when she swerved to bring the car back from the center line.

"If you'd stop being so aggravating, I could concentrate on driving. Take your choice."

"If I had a choice, *I'd* be driving," he responded. "Besides, there's not much more to tell. Doctors make a million notes and never let you read them. I'm to keep off the leg—take the pills he gave me—and have someone around to keep watch. Probably so that I don't fall out of bed on my head."

"Once was enough, huh?" She didn't let him lead her astray with that ploy. "Do you have to check back with him?"

"I told him that I was heading home tomorrow and that I'd see my own doctor for the follow-up."

"Tomorrow—I didn't know." She clutched the steering wheel as she heard his indrawn breath. "Sorry—I'm usually a good driver. You didn't tell me you were going home tomorrow."

"I hadn't planned on it. It seemed like a good way to escape the hospital's grip and there's not much else I can accomplish here. Horseback riding is also out of my agenda." There was a silence and he chuckled. "Too bad you don't have a ready-made excuse like that."

"If I'd known, I wouldn't have let you sling me into the shrubbery quite so fast. Incidentally, I meant to thank you earlier."

"Forget it."

"Mmmm." She chewed on her lip thoughtfully. "That doesn't solve the problems for tonight."

Drew kept his tone light. "I don't understand. What kind of problems?"

"Who's going to look after you when we get back to the lodge?" She darted a sideways glance at him before turning her attention back to the windshield. "Don't you see? You can't stay alone in your room— even if you could get up there. Didn't you say it was on the third floor?"

"Well, I could get it moved, I suppose." He rubbed his jaw as he thought about it. "But there isn't any twenty-four-hour nursing service, that's for sure. I'll just take my chances."

"What was the doctor worried about? Be serious, Drew."

"Something about circulation. If my leg turns black or green or chartreuse, or any intervening shade, I'm to get back to the hospital in a hurry. He's concerned about the first eight hours."

Despite his light tone, Lucie knew that Drew was concerned as well. "You're a blithering idiot—not staying in the hospital," she announced, forgetting that she'd only known him a matter of hours. "Since you didn't, you'll take my bed for tonight. I can pull that lounge in from the porch for me," she went on, not giving him a chance to object. "And you needn't offer any more caustic remarks about hourly health bulletins because it won't make any difference."

"Is it all right if I just say one thing?"

"I guess so." She scowled in his general direction. "What is it?"

"I just wanted to tell you that I appreciate all this." He straightened as if a load had been lifted from his shoulders. "Maybe I've been missing something all these years by being an only child."

Her lips quirked upward. "I'm in the same fix so I can't give you any advice. To be honest, that's one reason I was leery about meeting you today. I didn't know what to expect."

"But now look what's happened." He sounded thoroughly disgusted. "You're stuck doing night duty right off the bat."

"What's wrong with that? After trying to stay on top of that horse this afternoon, being horizontal sounds great."

"On that lounge mattress? Who are you kidding?"

"I don't anticipate being awake long enough to suffer, so you can stop flailing yourself. After all," she pointed out, "probably I'd have been run down by that crazy driver if you hadn't given me a shove into the shrubbery . . ." She broke off and started to laugh.

"Now what?" Drew wanted to know.

"I was just thinking how things change."

"Well, I find the present circumstances a lot more comfortable in some ways than earlier today," he went on musingly. "You made a big hit with my father, you know. I understand he's been after you to come and work in our place."

"He mentioned something about it . . ."

"But he didn't convince you?"

"I don't think that the market for furs is particularly good on the Arizona desert," she remarked wryly. "The retail field is all I know about."

"I'll admit that we don't stock mink coats in our gift shop. There are other things, though, if you insist on working."

"The corral, maybe?"

He chuckled at that. "Not yet. Receptionist? Tour guide? Ghost town expert?"

Lucie stopped, shaking her head at his last words. "Ghost town? That must be something new in your operation. It's the first I've heard of it."

"The restoration is still in the planning stage, although we hope to have the place functioning for the tourist invasion next spring. Actually, our ghost town is authentic—a remnant of the old Canyon Hill mine. The town's buildings aren't far from our lodge. We've kept the place fenced off all these years, but Dad's

convinced that we should go along with the current
interest in historical places. I've arranged to restore
part of it over the winter months."

"The ghost towns I've visited weren't very inspiring," Lucie said. "Most of them were full of terrible
Western souvenirs that were . . ."

"Made in Korea?"

She nodded. "And moldy museums next to hot dog
stands."

"Well, in ours we'll dispense with the hot dog stands
and let people have a peek at the mine shaft. The old
buildings will be reconstructed so the surroundings
will be authentic. There'll be a visitors' center with
food and gifts at the edge of the place—but more on
the order of a National Park facility."

"That sounds attractive. I insist on a free tour when
I come visiting."

"I can't tempt you to join our happy workers?" He
made his tone light but he was watching her through
narrowed eyes.

She shook her head, keeping her attention on the
road. "Nope. I'd be two bricks short of a load if I
took you on as my employer. It's better this way. Especially if we're to keep this splendid newfound
peace."

The irony in her tone didn't escape Drew. He chose
to ignore it for the moment. "Am I wrong or are those
the lights from Jackson Lake ahead of us?"

"I think you're right," Lucie replied, wishing that
he hadn't taken her refusal with such equanimity. He
could have argued a little or appeared downcast by
her decision—if he'd meant the offer in the first place.

She bit her lip as that possibility occurred to her, and the silence lengthened between them while the lights of the Jackson Lake resort complex grew steadily brighter.

She was turning off the road into the drive which led past the darkened corral and swimming pool when another thought suddenly came into her mind and she said abruptly, "You'll need pajamas—and a toothbrush. At least pajamas. I saw a brand-new toothbrush in my medicine cabinet, courtesy of the management. Should I drive by the lodge and go to your room for your belongings?"

"Not if you expect to find any pajamas," Drew said. "I don't use them. Is that going to bother you?"

"Well—er—of course not." She finally managed to get the last words out firmly. There was nothing unusual about the fact that a man didn't wear pajamas to bed, she told herself. On the other hand, there was no use pretending that she was accustomed to a six-foot man in her bedroom overnight even if he came complete *with* clothes. It took still longer to sound casual about one in his birthday suit.

"You missed the turnoff," Drew reminded her a minute or so later. "We *are* going to the cottage, aren't we?"

"Yes—certainly. It's hard to find the right lane at this time of night."

"*Isn't* it?" he agreed, managing to sound as if he believed her feeble excuse. He hesitated, searching for the right word, "There is one thing that still bothers me."

Lucie steeled herself. At that point, she was almost ready for anything. "What's that?"

"This car. I don't know how I'm going to get the damned thing home. The doctor outlawed driving completely. An airplane ticket is the only kind of transportation he'd okay." Drew shifted in the seat as she finally braked in front of the cottage. "I wonder if I could possibly impose on you for one more thing?" Then before she could even attempt to answer, he muttered, "Oh, hell! I can't ask you to change your plans any more than you already have. You've gotten the short end of this arrangement from the very beginning."

Lucie turned off the ignition with a decisive movement. "I told you that I could take care of myself. Would you mind letting me in on this—so I'll know what you're saving me from?" she added drily.

"Okay. I was going to ask if you'd cancel your other plans and drive this car south tomorrow. Since you're already headed for Arizona, a detour by our place shouldn't take more than an extra day or so of your time. Naturally, I'll be responsible for all your expenses and lodging. There shouldn't be any trouble postponing your hotel reservations further south. Of course, if driving alone bothers you—"

She cut in forcefully. "You make me sound like a Victorian heroine with the vapors. Why on earth should I mind two days driving on a perfectly good highway?"

"Well, if you're sure . . ."

"Of course," she told him. It wasn't until she was out of the car and going around to the other side to help him onto the path that she started having second thoughts. Somehow, in five seconds flat, she'd managed a complete about-face. What's more, she'd done it all on her own.

Even though the only illumination was the porch light of the cottage, Drew must have sensed her uncertainty. He remained by his door of the car to peer searchingly down at her. "Look, I won't hold you to it. If worst comes to worst, I'll send up somebody from the ranch to retrieve the car. I have no right to play free and easy with your plans."

If he'd argued, Lucie would have backtracked as gracefully as possible but his use of reverse psychology made mockery of her intentions. "No, really—it's quite all right," she assured him. "You should know that a woman has no trouble changing her mind. That's the easy part. I'll hold you to your promise about changing my reservations, though—and don't forget that I have to be back at my job by the end of the month."

"You'll be there with bells on. Damn it all! I'm getting stiffer all the time." He moved slowly and painfully up the path, hanging onto her shoulder.

"You should have stayed in the hospital," she scolded, scrabbling in her purse to find her key to the cottage. "At least I won't have any trouble getting you to stay in bed."

"From the way I feel, my only trouble will be getting out of it in the morning. Well, we'll face that when the time comes. I'll get the lights," he told her, reaching over the threshold after she unlocked the door.

Lucie led him across to the side of the bed. "I have an immersion heater in my luggage so I can make you a cup of tea or coffee in the dressing room while you're getting your clothes off." The offer was casually made and Lucie headed for the other room which adjoined the bath even before she heard him say, "Thanks, some tea would be fine." Once around the corner, she hesitated, wondering if she should have offered to help him remove his clothes and then decided against it. When Drew needed her assistance, he wouldn't hesitate to ask her for it. If her feminine instincts were to be trusted, she'd bet that he had plenty of aptitude and experience in that province. Probably his address book was full of females who'd happily dropped most everything to be with him for an evening.

Lucie chewed on her bottom lip as she thought about it. It was a good thing that her family relationship put her automatically out of the league.

Almost angrily, she reached for the immersion heater and went on into the bathroom to fill a mug with water before plugging the heater into the outlet beside the basin.

The telephone at the bedside rang just as the water began to boil. "Will you get it, please?" she called out, not wanting to leave the heater untended. "Tell whoever it is that I'll call them back."

Drew made an assenting noise from the other room and she heard him pick up the receiver to say "Hello" before she unplugged the heater. It took a while for her to ready a second cup of water and then brew the tea. She emerged from the dressing room with a mug in either hand, walking carefully so that the contents wouldn't spill.

Drew was in bed, propped up against the head-board with the sheet drawn up over his middle. Lucie kept her attention on the tea as she handed it to him, partly from necessity but mainly because she didn't want to stare at his broad tanned chest as he reclined against the pillows. "Did they leave a message?" she asked, trying to sound as if she really cared.

"Who? Oh, the phone call." He took a sip of the hot tea and sighed with satisfaction. "Tastes good."

"The phone call," she prompted, with a niggling feeling. "Who was it?"

"Long distance from San Francisco—somebody called Bruce." Drew glanced at her still figure by the bedside. "Friend of yours?"

"A man I work with." When there was no response, she went on reluctantly, "We've dated a few times. I'd forgotten that he was going to call."

"I guess he gathered that."

"Oh, Lord—did you say who you were? Explain—oh, you know . . ."

"I never thought of it." His eyebrows went up. "Should I?"

Her eyes sought her watch. "Well, it is almost mid-night. He probably wondered . . ."

"Wondered what?"

"What a man was doing in my room," she snapped, suspecting that Drew was enjoying the dialogue, "an-swering my phone."

Drew thought it over for a good three seconds. Then he shrugged. "Either he trusts you or he doesn't.

If he doesn't, there aren't enough explanations in the book to satisfy him. If he does—there's no need to say anything."

"That's all very well, but I hardly know the man. Something tells me that the acquaintance isn't going to reach maturity. I only hope . . ."

"Well?" Drew asked impatiently when her voice trailed off.

"That he doesn't noise it around at work."

Drew sat up, spilling some tea onto his chest in the process. "Dammit to hell," he said, brushing off the drops and leaning over to put the mug on the bed table before completing the mop-up operation. "If you want me to send a testimonial or give you a good conduct badge to take back to work with you, I'll be glad to do it."

"You needn't be insulting," Lucie interrupted, putting her own mug down forcefully on a bureau top. "I'm sorry that I mentioned it. I couldn't care less if I ever hear from the man again."

"That's just as well, because come to think of it, he didn't say anything about calling again." Drew scowled as she picked up his shirt and trousers from the back of a chair and started toward the dressing room. "What are you doing now?"

"First off, I'm going to hang up your clothes. Then I'm going out on the porch to bring in the lounge and put it in the dressing room. Why?"

"I'd appreciate a glass of water when you can get around to it." He was having trouble sounding properly humble. It was clear that he was more accustomed to ordering people than asking them, Lucie thought with some enjoyment. "I have to take these pills," he gestured toward a paper packet on the bed table at his elbow.

"Of course, I'll get it now."

"I can wait," he protested.

Lucie's glance went over him quickly. If she hadn't been so chary about staring at him in bed, she would have noticed earlier how tired he looked. From the tight way he was holding his jaw and the dark shadows under his eyes, it was evident that his leg was aching badly. "There's no need for you to wait," she told him gently and disappeared into the dressing room, taking just a minute to hang up his clothes before getting a glass of water from the bathroom. Carrying it back to the bedside, she reached for the pills and handed him two after reading the instructions on the envelope. She waited until he'd swallowed them with the water and went back to refill the glass, leaving it on the table beside him. "In case you're thirsty during the night."

He nodded and silently watched her pull in the redwood lounge from the porch. When she'd gotten it into the dressing room, he said, "Come and get one of these pillows. There's an extra blanket, too."

She walked back into the room and stared at him doubtfully. "I don't need the blanket—I can use my coat."

"Don't be a fool," he said, reaching down to shove the extra blanket toward her. "It feels like Jamaica in here. Probably I'll only keep a sheet on."

"Well, if you're sure." She gathered an extra pillow from the headboard and tucked the blanket under her arm. "I've set my alarm to check on you in three hours." When he opened his mouth to protest, she said calmly, "Save your breath. I've had a Red Cross first aid certificate for years and now I finally get to use it." Her lips curved in a smile. "I can't tell you how grateful I am."

Drew surveyed her from under half-lowered lids. "Just what kind of aid do you have in mind?"

"You should know that the patient is always the last to learn. Don't worry, if those pills do their work, you won't be bothered."

"And if you discover I'm at death's door, Miss Nightingale?"

"I promise to wake you up and tell you about it. Is there anything you want before I put out the light?" She reached for the switch but when he didn't answer, she looked at him over her shoulder. "Drew, you *are* all right, aren't you?"

"Yes, of course." He turned to punch up the pillow as if bored with the topic and slid down under the sheet. "Get some rest," he advised in a brusque tone, "or you'll feel like hell in the morning."

Lucie turned the light off without further comment, but she was remembering that other leavetaking near the corral when he wasn't so patently uninterested in her presence.

It took a while for her to get comfortable on the narrow lounge. After that, she dozed fitfully, afraid that she'd sleep through the alarm. As a result, the buzzer on her clock had barely erupted when she reached out to smother it. She groped for her robe at the foot of the bed and shrugged into it. Then she picked up the flashlight she'd carefully stashed away at bedtime.

She kept the beam on the floor as she crept into the bedroom, doing her best not to disturb Drew's quiet form. It wasn't until she got alongside the bed, that he startled her by reaching over to switch on the lamp, saying calmly, "I'm awake—you don't have to creep around."

Lucie didn't waste time on recriminations; instead, she put down the flashlight on the table and reached for his wrist. He allowed her thirty seconds to note his pulse rate, waiting until a relieved expression came over her face before he went on, "And the circulations's okay in my ankle, too, so you can relax."

She let out an audible sigh of relief. "I'm glad."

"Frankly, so am I. I don't mind a few aches but I'm all for happy endings. Right now, I feel like a fraud taking your bed. How about switching for the rest of the night?"

"You mean—I should move in here?" she asked, not quite sure how he meant it.

"That's right." He pushed up to a sitting position, keeping the sheet in place with his other hand. "I can take the lounge."

"No way." She put out a hand to stop him and then quickly pulled it back when she touched his bare shoulder. To cover her confusion, she said, "You stay right where you are."

He stared up at her, his eyes narrowed. "Well, there's plenty of room for both of us on this oversized mattress. I would have suggested it before, but . . ."

"Oh, no!" Lucie cut in, stricken that he'd gotten the

wrong idea. "I mean, I'm perfectly all right where I am."

"Don't you trust me?"

"It's not that. I might disturb you and it's vital that you get some rest."

"You wouldn't bother me a bit," he said, looking her over thoughtfully.

Lucie wondered if the tailored white cotton robe she had on over her equally tailored blue and white striped cotton pajamas had anything to do with his vehement denial. Illogically, it annoyed her. "Well, it would bother me," she snapped.

"I promise that I wouldn't move off this side of the bed."

"That wasn't what I meant at all."

There was a flicker of devilment in his gaze as he continued to stare at her. "Exactly what *did* you mean?"

"Merely that I'm going back to bed. In there," she said, pointing toward the dressing room so there could be no further misunderstanding. She hesitated and then bent over him to rest the back of her hand on his forehead. "I just wondered if you were running a fever."

"That's no excuse," he murmured.

She ignored that and straightened. "I'll get you some more water. It's time for your pills."

"Okay." It wasn't until she was back with the glass in her hand that he commented, "Maybe you'd better take an aspirin or something. Right now, you look as if you could use some rest."

"I am perfectly fine. *You* are the patient." There

was a perceptible edge to her voice as she shook two of the pills into his palm. She waited until he'd swallowed the medicine and replaced the glass on the table before she reached over to switch off the light. In her confusion, she forgot to retrieve the flashlight and collided painfully with the corner of the bureau as she swept back to the dressing room.

After that, it took her a good hour to get any sleep. She could vouch for the time because she spent the intervening sixty minutes staring angrily at the face of her travel alarm, listening to Drew's relaxed breathing as he slept in the next room.

Chapter

—4—

When Drew awoke the next morning, he was in just as disagreeable a mood as Lucie had been a few hours earlier.

He ached everywhere. Even his head felt as if an artillery regiment had scheduled a cannon barrage.

He groaned in protest, and opened his eyes slowly to see if that would help. It didn't—but he learned that the painful thuds he'd thought centered in his head had extended to the cottage door. Between knocks, there came the impatient rattle of a key. Drew's gaze focused on the keyhole, noting that there was a key on the inside which was apparently frustrating the intruder. He smiled with satisfaction and turned to go to sleep again when he remembered where he was and abruptly pushed up on an elbow.

One look at the undisturbed pillow by his side satisfied his doubts. He should have known, he thought. Then, as the sporadic knocking at the door resumed, he growled, "Damn it all—get lost!" There was no response to that except another series of knocks. He muttered something considerably more profane and got out of bed, grabbing the quilted bedspread from a nearby chair to cover his nakedness.

It wasn't an unqualified success but it did cover the vital parts. Drew was still trying to catch up the loose corner of the spread dragging on the floor as he reached the door and unlocked it.

The young chambermaid standing on the porch took an instinctive step backward when she found herself staring up at his forbidding form. "Good morning," she stammered, her cheeks flaming. Taking another look at the room assignment list clutched in her hand, she managed to say, "Miss Forsythe? I mean—I wondered if Miss Forsythe is checking out today."

Drew almost said, "I'll ask her when she wakes up," and then decided to preserve the family reputation. "My sister was up most of the night transporting me to the hospital in Jackson," he told the young woman. "I'll have her notify the front desk of her checkout plans as soon as possible."

The maid's embarrassment faded and she nodded. "Then I'll wait to clean the room—if that's all right."

"It might be better."

Drew's slow smile held such charm that the girl would have worked an extra shift if he'd asked. The color rose in her cheeks again. "Just call housekeeping whenever it's convenient," she told him breathlessly. "I can be over right away."

"Thanks, I appreciate it." Drew was closing the door when his gaze moved casually behind her. He stood unmoving for an instant and then he closed the door firmly, making sure the latch was in place. Back

inside, his glance swept the front of the room, checking that the drapes were completely closed on the
wide windows. Only then did he limp into the dressing
room, still clutching the bedspread absently around
his middle.

Lucie was sprawled face-down on the narrow
lounge. Sometime in the early morning, her pillow had
fallen or been pushed onto the floor and her blanket
was almost ready to join it. Drew stepped over both of
them as he reached down and shook her shoulder.

"Lucie—wake up!" When she muttered something
but didn't open her eyes, he persisted grimly. "Wake
up—you're about to have company."

That must have penetrated the outer reaches of her
consciousness. "Don' want cump'ny," she said and
burrowed firmly into the lounge pad.

Drew's lips tightened and he headed for the adjoining bathroom, dragging the bedspread behind him like
a train. An instant later, he tossed a palmful of cold
water on her prone figure. "*Now* will you get up?"

Lucie came upright so fast that she almost fell off
the lounge, even as she gasped, "Stop that! What a
miserable trick."

"Simmer down. You'll dry off." He reached over to
mop her face with an edge of the bedspread.

Lucie frowned up at him, clearly unable to believe
her eyes. "Why are you stomping around in that—
that—thing . . . ?"

"It's a fetish of mine. Bedspreads turn me on," he
snarled back, as angry by then as she was. "In case
you care, your boy friend is about to come calling."

"Vito? You mean *here?*" she squeaked.

"I sure as hell wouldn't be acting as town crier if he was just jogging around the block. Unless you want him to find you in this"—his gesture included the cluttered room—"I'd suggest you get something on."

"But what about you?" She reached for the blanket and sheet as his warning sank in. "You can't hang around in that thing."

Drew pulled up his bedspread and tossed a trailing end of it over his shoulder like a disdainful Roman centurion as he headed for the bathroom. His next words came from behind the door. "I don't know what the devil you have against bedspreads but I'm now going to take a shower and then I'll switch to a towel. I hope that makes you feel better."

Lucie reached out and clutched the edge of the door before he could close it completely. "What if he hears the water?" she hissed desperately as a rapping from the front door came on cue.

Drew put his head around the door far enough to watch her struggle into her robe. "Just tell him you're about to get into the shower," he whispered back. "Then he won't drag his feet. You'd better answer the door, though. If he has to hang around out there much longer, the maid will come back. It would be better if they didn't compare notes." With that ominous comment, he closed the door. An instant later, the water in the shower was turned on, full force.

"Good God, you mean the maid knows you're here? Oh, damn!" Lucie's last words came as another fusillade of knocks sounded. "I'm coming—I'm coming. Hold on, will you?" She managed to smile as she unlocked the front door. "Vito! What a surprise!"

Her performance wouldn't have won an academy award but Vito wasn't critical.

"Lucinda—*cara*." His glance took in her robe and tousled hair. "I disturbed you? I'm so sorry. But you were at the door just a minute ago."

"I was? I mean—yes, of course, I was," she corrected herself quickly.

"I came to see how you were feeling and to arrange our day." He looked pointedly past her. "Maybe we could discuss it."

Lucie stayed where she was. "I was just adjusting my shower. As a matter of fact—the water's still running."

"Turn it off. I'll wait here."

She opened her lips to protest and closed them again at his stubborn expression. "All right," she said. "Just give me a minute." Marching to the bathroom door, she opened it and went inside. She slid her hand around the edge of the shower curtain—ignoring the startled gasp from the man inside the tub as she turned off the mixing faucet and hurriedly left the room.

Vito had improved his position in the interval and was standing just inside the front door, waiting for her. "Now—about today—" he said, beaming. "How long will it take you to be ready for breakfast?"

"About a half hour," Lucie said firmly, opening the front door with a gesture that he couldn't mistake. "Shall I meet you in the dining room?"

"If you like." He looked back over his shoulder toward the dressing room, puzzled. "Do I still hear water running?"

Lucie closed her eyes, wishing she could close her hands around Drew McLaren's neck at that particular instant. "I'm trying to get some really hot water—I left it running in the basin."

"I'll complain about it at the front desk as soon as I get back to the lodge," he promised.

"Honestly, it isn't necessary . . ."

"No trouble at all. A half hour then—in the dining room." He hesitated on the porch. "Is that your car?"

His gaze was on the black car parked directly in front of the cottage. Lucie tried for a plausible answer. "Sort of. I'll explain when I see you at breakfast," she said, before closing the door on his heels.

A moment later, Drew appeared in the bathroom doorway with a towel wrapped around his middle. "Remind me to buy you a new razor blade. Most people throw them away after the second year."

"Don't give me any ideas," she said, glaring back at him as he tried to stop the blood seeping from a nick on his chin. "Even a dull one would work for what I have in mind."

"Temper—temper." He turned back to the basin and continued with his shaving, leaving the door partway open. "You'll learn to roll with the punches if you flaunt convention like this."

"Very amusing. My social life doesn't usually start at—" she searched for the travel alarm and read the dial—"nine-thirty! Good Lord, is it that late?" She bit her lip as other details came to mind. "How do you feel?"

"Better—before I started shaving."

"I didn't mean that. I'm talking about your leg."

She was trying not to stare at the towel covering it. "How is it?"

"Okay. I'll be out of here shortly." Drew started to close the bathroom door, just as another series of knocks came from the front one.

His "Dammit, *now* what?" merged with Lucie's "Oh, Lord—who can that be?"

"Probably somebody to install a traffic light," Drew said as they stared at each other grimly. Then he flipped an imaginary coin. "You're on," he announced. "Clothes make the difference. I wonder if I'll have to spend the entire morning in this bathroom."

"Not if I have anything to say about it," she promised and marched to the front door, swinging it open. "What do you want now—"

Her voice faded as she found an attractive blonde in her early thirties standing on the porch. The stranger, who looked equally astounded at seeing Lucie, recovered her poise first. "Miss Forsythe? I'm sorry to bother you. I'm Paula Bennett." When Lucie's puzzled expression didn't change, the other went on drily. "Drew's secretary. I'm afraid I've misplaced my boss. He told me he was coming to meet you and that's his car outside—but nobody's seen him since yesterday. Do you know if something's happened?" She paused, obviously waiting for an explanation.

"Yes—well, actually not in the way you think," Lucie said, stumbling over the words and wondering what Drew would want her to say. "He hurt his leg last night and I drove him into the hospital in Jackson."

"Oh, heavens! Is he all right? I wish you'd let me know."

"How could I? I didn't know where you were." Lucie's eyes narrowed in sudden suspicion. "As a matter of fact—where *were* you?"

"Waiting around in the lodge after nine o'clock. Drew could have told you," Paula said, running a hand through her close-cropped platinum hair which gave her an attractive gamine look.

Lucie drew in her breath. "I see," she said ominously.

"I don't think you do," Drew replied, appearing in the dressing room behind her. "Come in, Paula. I gather you've met Lucie." He was pulling the hanger with his clothes on it from the closet as he spoke. "Find a place to sit down while I get dressed. I've had this towel on for so long I feel like a football player in a television commercial."

His secretary's brows went up in surprise but her voice was under control when she asked, "How long have you been here?" Then, before he could reply, she turned to Lucie apologetically, "My boss doesn't usually make a habit of drop-in visits."

Drew paused in the process of closing the bathroom door. "Remind me to raise your salary, Paula." He gave Lucie a slanted grin. "Something tells me that Vito wouldn't have been so understanding."

"I have no intention of putting it to the test," she managed to reply before the door shut behind him. She followed Paula into the bedroom, watching the other woman survey the furnishings. "Now that we have a chaperone, I can open the curtains."

The secretary smiled at her over her shoulder and sat down in an upholstered chair by the desk. "Sunshine always makes things look better. From the conversation, I gather that it's been a rough night."

"The night wasn't so bad but the morning's been a little hectic." Lucie tightened the belt on her robe as she leaned against the wall by the window. "Drew forgot to mention that you were here."

"He's not a man to volunteer information." Paula was making no attempt to hide her curiosity. "He didn't tell me much about you either—just that his father was remarrying and that his stepmother had a daughter. He must have been pleased to discover that you were such a beauty."

Color mounted in Lucie's cheeks at the compliment. It hadn't taken long for her to realize that the same adjective could be applied to Drew's secretary. Paula Bennett had a clear blue-eyed gaze and a lovely Nordic complexion to go with her pale hair. Her mouth was a little too wide for classic beauty and her curves were too pronounced for high fashion, but she would have drawn attention from any man within range.

Paula was going on in her crisp but not unpleasant tones, "You appear to have gotten very well acquainted in the interval. Drew's hasty exit in the towel reminded me of that old joke . . ."

Lucie frowned. "What old joke?"

"Where the mayonnaise jar says to the refrigerator, 'Close the door, dear—I'm dressing,' " Paula said irrepressibly.

There was a groan behind them as Drew entered in

time to hear her comment. "You'll have to forgive my secretary," he told Lucie. "She has an offbeat sense of humor. Frankly, I think she was weaned on Marx Brothers movies." Turning to the other woman, he announced calmly, "If you don't forget about the towel —you *can* forget about the raise I mentioned."

Paula shrugged amiably. "One towel—absolutely forgotten."

"Fair enough." He gestured toward the trousers he was wearing which still showed the effects of rolling around in the shrubbery the night before. "Besides, I'm the one to pump for the evening's gory details. Lucie's too diplomatic to mention them."

By then, Lucie was tired of being ignored. "One detail I *have* noticed is that he seldom lets me get a word in," she told Paula. "But now—if you'll excuse me, I'll get dressed. Vito's expecting me at the lodge for breakfast and I'm already late. I'm happy to have met you, Miss Bennett . . ."

"Mrs. Bennett," Drew corrected her as he walked over to the bed table and picked up his packet of pills.

"Mrs. Bennett," Lucie apologized, wondering why she felt relieved to hear it. Probably it just meant that Paula was widowed or divorced. Few husbands would agree to their wives traveling around the country in such fashion—especially not if the employers looked like Drew McLaren. Lucie's lashes lifted then and she brought her gaze up to meet his. "Since Mrs. Bennett is here, you won't need my help with the car and I can keep my plane reservation. I'll call you before I leave, though . . ."

"Whoa—take it easy," he cut in when she stopped to take a breath. "Nothing's changed. Paula can't help with the car. She doesn't drive."

"Doesn't drive?" She turned and stared at Paula. "How did you get here?"

A thin smile flickered over the other woman's face. Then she raised her arms to shoulder level and fluttered them gracefully. "A seven-thirty flight to Jackson and the lodge bus from there," she reported.

"I'm sorry," Lucie said, biting her lip, "I didn't think." She rounded on Drew. "All right, then. I'll talk to you about it later. Will you be in your room?"

"Probably. If not, I'll leave word with the switchboard." He looked around, obviously checking the bedroom to see if he'd left anything behind. "We'll go now and give you some peace."

"Wait a minute—" Lucie said, remembering what had been bothering her. "You can't walk all the way up to the lodge and if Paula can't drive—" She took a deep breath. "I'll hurry and throw some clothes on."

"There's no need," Drew cut in. "To make an extra trip, I mean. The doctor said that I should start exercising my leg today—Paula can prop me up on the way if I get tired." He opened the door and motioned his secretary to precede him outside. "We'll see you later."

He and Paula had walked some fifty feet down the deserted track toward the lodge when she looked around and commented, "I'd say there was a storm brewing. What do you think?"

Drew squinted overhead and then turned a puzzled face toward her. "You're crazy. There isn't a cloud in the sky and from the way the sun feels, the thermometer will probably hit seventy-five."

"Maybe, but I still feel uneasy."

Drew started to argue and saw her mischievous expression. "Oh, you mean family relations might be a little strained in days to come?"

"Uh-huh. About the time Lucie discovers that I have a perfectly good driver's license." She pursed her lips. "If I work things right, I can blackmail you long enough to take care of all my Christmas presents."

"So much for that helpless widow role of yours," Drew told her cheerfully as he limped along. "It's a good thing that Walt's going to shackle you with a new wedding ring next month."

"I think so myself, but what does that have to do with my blackmail?"

"As treasurer of the McLaren corporation he wouldn't want his wife sentenced for extortion. I suggest that you give up a life of crime."

"What do you suggest instead?"

"How about breakfast—I'll pick up the check."

"I had every intention of charging it to you anyhow. It's nice being engaged to your financial adviser. He gives me all sorts of handy tips to save my budget—" She broke off her teasing when she saw that her employer was really not paying close attention. "Look, Drew, you can tell me to hush up if I'm making waves," she said, putting a hand on his arm, "but I'd appreciate knowing what's going on."

"I'm not sure myself. Call it a hunch if you like, but it seemed like a good idea to keep my brand-new 'sister' at close range for a while."

"For business or personal reasons?"

He grinned. "Maybe a little bit of both. The folks wanted her to be around when they returned from their honeymoon and the accident last night provided an excuse."

Paula's clear gaze met his. "Did you report the driver?"

"There wasn't even a jackrabbit within a half mile—let alone any authority. Probably it was some drunk letting off steam."

"I suppose you're right. Do you want me to keep Lucie company on the drive south?"

Drew frowned. "I wish you could, but it would look as fishy as hell. Right now, she has you cast as my private, very confidential secretary. It would be out of character if you turned into a chaperone."

"I shouldn't have mentioned spending the night at the lodge," Paula sounded rueful. "Never mind, I'll make it clear eventually that our adjoining rooms are complete with locks on the doors. And then if I tell her about Walter—that should clear away any obstacles."

"Which is precisely why I don't want you to do any explaining about locked doors or fiancés. We'll let Lucie drive to the ranch alone with her suspicions."

Paula stared up at his determined face. He was trying not to favor his injured leg but she could tell it was paining him more than he let on. One reason she had always gotten along well with him in the past was because she had never attempted to broach the barriers of his personal life. She knew that Drew would tolerate only so much questioning before an austere expression would descend and mask his feelings. After that, any discussion was a waste of time. "May I offer the opinion that you're not going to win any brownie points with Lucie if she thinks that we're sharing more than a breakfast table at the lodge," Paula said finally.

"The thought had occurred to me."

"But you don't want to change your mind?"

His jaw firmed. "Not now."

"So be it," she said with a sigh. "I'm glad Walter isn't complicated. You'd better make sure that he and Lucie don't eventually compare notes or we'll both be in trouble." Paula directed a sideways glance at Drew as they started up the lodge steps. "In fact, I certainly hope that you know what you're doing."

Vito Perelli said almost exactly the same words a half hour later as he leaned across a breakfast table in the lodge dining room and spoke to Lucie. "Why should you have to bother with that man's car?" he went on afterward. "Drew McLaren can hire somebody to drive it to Arizona for him—or he can send an employee from that hotel of his. There's enough help around to transport a fleet of cars."

"Maybe he wants his employees on the job," Lucie said flippantly. "My hourly rate is cheaper. Actually, I don't mind very much. I was practically going by the front door on my way to Phoenix." Since Paula and Drew had left the cottage, she had, for a reason that didn't bear closer inspection just then, decided that it might be interesting to spend a night or so at the McLaren resort. It would simply postpone reaching her real destination, she had assured herself. Which wasn't a calamity.

At that moment, she was already wishing herself on the journey. And that was ridiculous considering her elegant surroundings. The mammoth view windows of the dining room provided a panorama of the famous Tetons, whose rocky gray outlines with a capping of snow were spectacular on such a clear day. The walls of the room were covered with murals which showed the Wyoming country as it was when first explored. Colorful panels depicted hunters, "bullboating" wagons on the rivers, and the trading fairs which provided trappers with supplies for survival through the severe winters.

Lucie's glance returned to the man sitting across the table from her and she almost laughed at the blatant contrast. It was hard to imagine a person less suited to rugged pioneering life than Vito Perelli. From his sleek dark hair to his navy blue sport shirt and slacks worn with a white linen blazer, there wasn't a discordant note in his appearance. At any moment, Lucie half expected him to turn to an admiring audience and extoll the benefits of the newest sports car or detergent. Her pulse automatically accelerated as he fixed his high-voltage gaze on her.

"Maybe you'll change your mind and spend your whole vacation at McLaren's," he mused. "Actually it might work out very well."

Her eyebrows went up. "For whom?"

"Me, of course. One learns to list the priorities in life. I plan to be down that way concluding some business."

She gave him an amused look as she sipped coffee. "Well, I haven't worked out a list, but I think an overnight stay will do nicely. Besides—you're a paying guest and that's different from a member of the family. You know that saying about relatives or fish after they're on the premises for three days."

"I don't bother with such things. We could check with Drew about your welcome if you're worried. He's coming in now with a blonde in tow. I thought you said he wasn't feeling well."

Lucie resisted an urge to look over her shoulder. "He bruised his leg, that's all."

"He *is* limping. There doesn't seem to be much else wrong with him. That blonde is prime property."

Lucie frowned and risked a quick glance over her shoulder. Drew and Paula were chatting amiably with the hostess as she seated them at a window table. "The prime property," Lucie said, her inflection showing what she thought of Vito's description, "is Paula Bennett—Drew's secretary."

"Better and better. She does look familiar. I must have seen her around the resort in Arizona. What's she doing here?"

"I didn't ask."

Vito's smile flashed at her dry response. "You should. It's easier to get answers that way. Of course, they're not always what you want to hear. More coffee?"

"No, thanks." Lucie blotted her lips with her napkin and put it on the table. "I have to go and pack. Are you checking out today, too?"

"Tomorrow. I'll catch an early plane." He leaned closer. "You could persuade me to change my plans without trouble. I'm an excellent chauffeur and, in this case, I'd work without pay."

"No salary at all?" She pretended to be impressed.

He shrugged. "Possibly a few side benefits—that's all."

"Exactly what I was afraid of," she said, laughing. "If you're on a business trip, you can't spare the time for such shenanigans."

"That's a new description for what I had in mind," he admitted, putting his hand over hers. "I want to know you better, Lucie. Did you think I'd be satisfied with a breakfast date and a good-by kiss?"

"To be honest, I hadn't gotten any further than the bacon and eggs," she said, deciding that his assurance needed taking down a peg.

His grip tightened for an instant, then he patted her fingers smartly and withdrew his hand to light a cigarette. "When you know me better, you will learn."

She saw no point in arguing about such an unlikely possibility. "It must be nice to work in a business without a fixed schedule," she said, changing the subject. "Are all import business firms like that or are you just lucky?"

"I don't know about other firms. You needn't think that because I have some free time that I don't work hard." He tapped his forehead. "This part, for example, seldom stops."

Lucie came to the conclusion that even a free breakfast paled before such a monumental ego. Why was it, she wondered irrelevantly, that splendid profiles were seldom accompanied by a sense of humor. She reached for her purse and pushed her chair back. "Vito, I can't thank you enough for breakfast and for being so nice about our dinner date last night."

He gestured expansively. "It is nothing. Now—about driving down to Arizona . . ."

She shook her head. "Thanks, but I've really made other plans. There are some friends I plan to visit on the way." She crossed her fingers surreptitiously under the folds of her wrap skirt, a little amazed at her new-found aptitude for lying in her teeth. "From the sound of things, we'll run into each other at McLaren's." As he bunched his napkin and pushed back his own chair, she protested, "Don't you want to finish your breakfast? There's no need for you to see me back to the cottage."

"I've had enough—of some things." He tacked on the last words so there was no mistaking his meaning. "Come—let's say hello to your new brother and his girl friend."

"Secretary."

"That, too." Vito kept a tight grip on her elbow so that Lucie couldn't have chosen another exit from the dining room even if a trapdoor had yawned at her feet.

He marched her through the tables over to the one she wanted to avoid by the window. "Drew, I'm sorry to hear you are not well," he said in a jovial tone when they reached it. "No, don't get up—I insist."

" 'Morning, Vito. Lucie," Drew's casual nod included both of them as he settled back in his chair. "Paula, I don't think you've met Mr. Perelli. Mrs. Bennett works with me, Vito."

"So Lucie said." Vito bent over Paula's hand with every evidence of pleasure. "I'm sure I've seen you at McLaren's when I've stayed there in the past."

"Probably—although Drew doesn't let me out of the office as often as I'd like. Lucie, I love your outfit. Sit down and tell me where you bought it."

"I'd like to, but I'm on my way to the cottage to get packed. Make Vito join you for another cup of coffee, though. The poor man feels compelled to walk me back and it really isn't necessary. Especially since we'll all be seeing each other in a day or so."

Vito hesitated, clearly torn between the lingering leavetaking he'd planned on Lucie's doorstep and Paula's attractive figure just across the table. His expression revealed his dilemma but finally the bird in hand, literally, won. He released Paula's fingers and turned to kiss Lucie. "Cara, I'm desolate that you're determined to leave so soon."

As graceful as his gesture was, Lucie managed to sidestep at the final moment and the kiss, which was destined for her lips, glanced off her cheekbone. "Ciao, Vito." Her smile faded as she turned to find Drew glowering at her. "Any last words or instructions before I hit the road?" she asked him. "Maybe you'd like to check my driver's license?" She was simply babbling from nervousness and Drew's glance showed that he knew it.

He didn't make the same mistake. "We'll have a room ready for you when you arrive. If you have any trouble on the road, just call the lodge. Someone will get word to me."

Lucie nodded, wishing she could tell him to take

care of his leg and arrange an appointment with his doctor as soon as he arrived home. She clamped down on the words, knowing how scornfully he'd greet that suggestion. All three of them were watching her by then, and she put a hand up to her hot cheek, aware that she was acting like a guest who lingers too long on the doorstep after the party is over. She summoned a bright smile. "Well, I'll be going, then. See you all in a day or so."

She left the room, knowing the only noteworthy thing about her departure was that she managed to avoid colliding with any of the waiters on her way to the door.

Chapter
-5-

After such a leavetaking, it wasn't strange that Lucie felt reluctant to renew acquaintances when she finally turned into the drive of McLaren's resort complex three days later. The same reluctance had prompted her to linger longer than necessary in Salt Lake City and on the road. Near the border of Arizona, she discovered that while summer might have been disappearing in Wyoming, it still stayed with a vengeance farther south. The thermometer climbed and Lucie issued silent thanks for the car's air-conditioning system.

The passing scenery proved so interesting that the driving turned out to be a pleasure rather than the chore she'd anticipated. After an impulsive detour to view the wonders of Bryce Canyon, she finally headed for Flagstaff and then turned north on the road to the Grand Canyon.

A discreet signpost with the single word McLAREN lettered on it came into view just south of the National Park boundary. Lucie was tempted to drive on and renew her acquaintance with the grandeurs of the Canyon she'd visited on an earlier trip. Common sense prevailed and she turned on the hard-surfaced road leading to the McLaren resort. Sooner or later, she'd have to make an appearance and there was no point in postponing it. She only hoped that Drew hadn't needed the car earlier. Then she recalled the way he'd shanghaied her into service like a modern-day Captain Bligh, and she decided not to apologize for her late arrival.

The early afternoon sun beat down on the car from an almost cloudless sky that was a marvelous blue, undimmed by the smoke and haze Lucie had noted on her drive the day before. Since leaving Flagstaff, she'd passed miles of piñon juniper, which provided dark green coloring for the arid landscape. The grasses growing rank at the tree roots covered all shades of brown and gray. Brighter color came from the yellow daisies which bloomed everywhere. Along the road to the resort, she found that they had competition from the cliffrose shrubs, a shaggy twisted evergreen with cream-colored flowers. Lucie slowed down to admire them, recalling that Indian warriors had used the wood for arrow shafts while their women had shredded the bark for diapers and used it to line their papoose cradleboards.

Another curve of the road brought McLaren's resort into view and she drew a breath of pleased surprise. It was a far bigger complex than she'd anticipated, blending into the desert landscape with an ease that showed a master designer's touch. The main lodge was of weathered adobe-type brick, capped with a tile roof. Shrubbery softened the building outlines and a restful fountain served as focal point for the curving entrance drive. Lucie caught glimpses of an inner garden and swimming pool through the brick patio arches at either side of the lodge. As she turned into the entranceway, a small sign indicated a parking lot beyond the main loading sector and directions for the corral and shop areas. For an instant, she wondered if she should park the car down there and then realized that she was simply stalling again. Deliberately she drove up in front of the main entrance and turned off the ignition.

When a smiling bellman came out to the car, he greeted her before she could say a word.

"Miss Forsythe? Welcome to McLaren's. You can go right in." He opened the car door for her and was retrieving her garment bag from the back seat. "I'll get your bags in the trunk."

"Thanks. I'd appreciate it." Lucie handed over the keys and followed him around the car. "How did you know . . ." she began hesitantly.

He didn't let her finish. "Who you were? That's easy. All of us know Mr. McLaren's car."

"Oh, of course," she said, feeling foolish.

"With a very pretty, brown-haired lady driving it. Those were Mr. McLaren's exact words. I think he's in his office if you want to see him. Your bags will be taken to your room right away."

"But the car . . ."

"We'll take care of it." He placed her two bags on the step and gestured toward the carved wooden doors of the lodge entrance. "Just ask for Mr. McLaren at the front desk."

"Thank you, I will." For a moment, Lucie wondered if she should tip him, but he was in the car and driving away before she could open her purse.

Her glance was thoughtful as she went into the spacious, shaded lobby. There was an atmosphere of quiet, solid comfort reflected by the tasteful furniture groupings around a Spanish-style fireplace, the marvelous design of Indian rugs on the waxed tile floors, and banks of palms in terra cotta containers near the doors leading to the patio. An inviting gift shop was at the far end of the lobby and a corridor beyond the reception area evidently led to a dining room.

She walked over to the front desk and spoke to an Indian woman who was sorting mail. "Could you tell me where I can find Mrs. Bennett?" she asked, still postponing the inevitable.

"She's in the administrative offices—a building just beyond the hotel." The woman reached for a telephone. "If I could tell her your name . . ." She paused politely.

"Forsythe. Lucinda Forsythe."

The receptionist looked puzzled for a moment and then she checked a list on a clipboard nearby. "Yes, of course, Miss Forsythe. But Mr. McLaren left instructions that he was to be notified as soon as you arrived. Did you particularly want to see Mrs. Bennett first?"

"No—it isn't necessary. There's really no need for me to bother Mr. McLaren either. If you could just tell me which room I'm to have . . ."

Her plea fell on deaf ears. "Mr. McLaren asked specifically to be called," the receptionist said, her fingers already busy on the telephone dial. She waited for the connection and then said into the mouthpiece, "It's Anna here, Mr. McLaren. Miss Forsythe has arrived. Yes, of course, I'll tell her." She hung up and turned back to Lucie. "He's on his way over and wants you to wait, please. Henry, take Miss Forsythe's things up to the family suite." The last order was given to a young bellman who had just arrived, wheeling Lucie's suitcases and garment bag on a cart.

The family suite! Lucie's imagination reeled and her plans of staying in a modest room before leaving on the first transportation south in the morning went glimmering. She managed to smile her thanks at the receptionist, trying to look as if she was accustomed to family suites and people vying to carry her bags.

The prospect of meeting Drew again didn't add to her peace of mind, and she walked over to inspect a planting of succulents near the wall, trying to look engrossed in their botanical labels.

It didn't take the firm footsteps behind her to advertise Drew's presence; Lucie's instincts told her he was in the room. She took a deep breath, keeping her attention on a barrel cactus in front of her. Then, abruptly, she felt herself being turned to face him.

"Where in the hell have you been?" Drew chipped out the words like slivered ice. "I was about to call the State Patrol and have them put out an APB."

His attack caught Lucie unaware. "What on earth for?" she got out finally. "I wasn't lost. You should have told me you were in a hurry for the car."

"The car be damned! You had enough time to get here and halfway back to Jackson again."

"Not and observe the speed limit. I *did* go see

Bryce Canyon," she confessed. "It seemed silly not to since I was driving right past."

"I suppose it never occurred to you to phone and report that you were still alive." He raked a hand through his hair. "Your mother would have been frantic if I'd admitted I hadn't heard from you."

"Good Lord, I don't see why. I certainly didn't report to my mother at five-minute intervals before she was married, and I can't think that your father keeps very close tabs on you." Her eyes narrowed as she stared up at him. "Did you ever tell him about hurting your leg?"

"There was no need. Paula made me check with the doctor when we got back. It's mending fine."

From what Lucie could see, he certainly didn't look as if he was close to the last rites. His beige gabardine slacks were immaculate and he was wearing a blue oxford cloth shirt that was without a wrinkle. The shirt was short-sleeved, revealing the muscles across his shoulders and his deeply tanned arms. He gestured her toward the elevator. "Your room's on the second floor. Come along—I'll see you settled in. You look as if you needed a cool shower or a dip in the pool."

Lucie knew that her pale yellow slacks had a few wrinkles in them but she'd just congratulated herself that her matching print overblouse looked almost as fresh as when she'd put it on that morning. Even the soft Italian leather espadrilles which had taken such a frightening bite of her budget were polished and unblemished. She'd dressed carefully so that she wouldn't arrive at McLaren's looking like an Albanian refugee, but if Drew's disparaging tone was anything to go by, she hadn't been noticeably success-ful. Well, she was damned if she'd let him see her chagrin.

"A bath sounds marvelous," she said, following him to the elevator. "I'm enjoying this sunshine, though. We haven't seen enough of it in San Francisco lately. Did I say something amusing?" she asked stiffly, seeing his shoulders start to shake with laughter as the elevator doors closed behind them.

"Not really. Your mother would be proud of you. If you need a safe topic—there's always the weather. Don't you think we know each other well enough by now that we could get on to more interesting things?"

As the elevator stopped, she waited for the doors to open and then followed Drew down an attractive, car-peted corridor until he pulled up in front of a door and reached for a key. "It's hard to keep up with your disposition," she commented drily. "A minute ago you were taking my head off for not punching a time clock. It's strange—your father seems such a pleasant person."

Her appraisal didn't appear to daunt him. "And I'm sure your mother is very nice," he said blandly. "I've enjoyed talking to her on the phone. Go on in," he gestured her ahead of him as he opened the door, re-vealing a comfortable sitting room furnished in restful earth tones.

Lucie walked slowly over to the wide windows along one side and discovered a wrought iron balcony which overlooked the hotel's inner patio and pool.

"There's a kitchenette over there. Your bedroom's through here." Drew indicated an open door on the other side of the sitting room. "There's another bedroom beyond and a bath connecting them. I hope you don't mind sharing the facilities—I promise you'll find the bed better than that lounge in Jackson."

Lucie ignored his last words to concentrate on the first part of his announcement. "What do you mean—sharing?"

"Just that. This is the family suite. I live here, too. Naturally there'll be other arrangements made when the folks get back. Dad said something about their preferring a guesthouse, but he wants your mother to decide."

She waved that aside. "I'd be perfectly fine in a single room. There's no need for me to inconvenience you."

"It's no trouble. I'm seldom around so you won't have to worry about running into me. Just call room service if you'd like anything now. We'll have dinner downstairs about seven if that suits you. I'll see if Paula's free to come here and join us for cocktails around six-thirty. Now, if you'll excuse me, there's some phoning I have to do."

"Of course." She watched him head down a short hall to the bedroom beyond the one she was to occupy. For an instant, she wondered if she should ask permission to monopolize the bath and decided against it. When the bedroom door closed behind him, her lips tightened. Obviously he wasn't giving her even a second thought. Now that she was safely in the fold and his car was unscathed, Drew's mind was on more vital things.

She closed the door to the bedroom he'd allotted

her more forcefully than necessary and then felt sorry
afterward when she saw her elegant surroundings. The
curtains, rug, and bedspread on the king-sized bed,
were all light beige. Grasscloth in a similar tone was
on the wall bchind the oak headboard, and cinnamon
linen covered the upholstered chairs by the writing
desk and bureau. A sliding window was a continua-
tion of those in the sitting room and opened out onto
the iron balcony she'd noticed earlier.

Lucie saw that her bags had been placed on luggage
racks near the closet and she put her purse atop the
bureau before walking over to peer cautiously around
the bathroom door.

Copper tile and beige fixtures complemented the
cinnamon accent of the bedroom—even to rust-
colored towels on the racks. Lucie gave the furnishings an appreciative but cursory glance since her
interest just then was on the bedroom beyond. She
went across the tiled floor on tiptoe and pushed the
bolt on the far door.

Then she bent and turned on the taps in the tub before going back to her bedroom to take off her
clothes. A few minutes later, she reentered the
bathroom in her travel robe to pour some fragrant
bubble bath under the faucet and watched it froth.

She slid out of her robe and dropped it on the top
of a decorative hamper close by. After carefully getting into the tub, she let out a sigh of sheer bliss as she
relaxed in the scented water.

She decided to soak for a bit while she planned how
to cope with Drew on his home ground. There was no
sound from his adjoining bedroom, but she moved

carefully in the water; having to share a bath again did nothing to further her hopes of a cool, aloof relationship.

They'd been pitched into an intimacy almost from the first, she mused, and it didn't appear that things were going to get any better. If anything, his regard seemed to be going downhill. The day they'd met, she could have sworn he was going to kiss her at the corral. A few minutes ago when he'd come upon her in the lobby, she'd been greeted with all the warmth of an Internal Revenue agent who'd arrived for an unexpected audit of the company books.

It wasn't that Drew was incapable of exhibiting masculine charisma—magnetism came as naturally as breathing to the man. All he had to do was walk through a room and every woman within sight looked as if she'd discovered prime rib among the hamburger.

Her stepfather hadn't commented on Drew's appearance, but it was strange that her mother hadn't seen fit to exhibit a picture sometime during the courtship. Her new husband certainly must have shown her one. Anyone would think that it had almost been a conspiracy between them.

Lucie sat upright and reached for a washcloth that she'd left on the edge of the tub. It was time to stop mooning and come back to reality, she told herself.

She had just picked up a cake of soap when she suddenly sat immobile. Slowly, almost painfully, her glance moved to the nearby basket hamper and her robe on the tiled floor.

Just an instant before, she'd caught a glimpse of the nylon wrap as it slithered from the hamper lid to the floor. She stared fixedly at the hamper again, trying to reassure herself that she'd probably discarded the robe carelessly atop it in the first place. Either that, or a sudden draft had nudged it over the edge.

"But that's silly," she muttered, unaware that she'd said it aloud. "There isn't any draft because the window isn't open and the fan isn't on."

Even as she spoke, there was movement on Drew's side of the room and his voice came through the closed bathroom door. "Are you talking to me?"

Lucie ducked under the protective layer of bubbles on hearing him and felt like an utter fool as realization dawned. She sat up again, saying, "Sorry. I was just thinking out loud."

There was a masculine snort which didn't need translating—even through the door—and footsteps receded. Color flooded Lucie's cheeks, and she hurriedly retrieved the soap which had slipped down into the water.

She had just replaced it in the soap dish when she heard a strange rustling noise in the room. For a moment she thought she had imagined it. Then she shot a suspicious look at the door leading to Drew's bedroom. Her reaction was not surprising because there obviously wasn't any distracting element in the bathroom itself; the spout of the tub wasn't dripping, and there wasn't any water coming from the modern basin across the room. Then, belatedly, she recalled that the noise wasn't across the room—it was considerably closer. Which could only mean the hamper against the wall—practically at arms length. Gingerly she levered herself up to survey it more closely.

Lucie had no idea of what an appealing figure she presented in the long mirror above the vanity on the opposite wall. The iridescent soap bubbles clung to her, accentuating every lovely curve as she perched on the edge of the tub and gazed warily at the hamper. Silence reigned in the room for a full thirty seconds. "Damn and double damn," she thought in exasperation when nothing happened. The only thing wrong was an overactive imagination on her part and she'd be courting a case of pneumonia if she sat there dripping much longer.

Then, just so she could relax completely, she reached over and lifted the cover on the hamper.

A split second later, she'd slammed it down again so fast that it was almost a continuous action. "Drew," she screamed desperately, pushing on the cover so hard that her knuckles were white with strain. "For God's sake—come in here!"

"What's the matter?"

She heard his answering call at the same time the door across the room vibrated against the bolt. "Come the other way," she shouted. "That door's open. Oh, please hurry!"

She heard footsteps pound down the hall and moments later, the door from her bedroom burst open.

"What in the devil's going on——" he exclaimed, seeing her crouched by the hamper, clad only in soap bubbles and goose bumps.

Her lack of attire was the least of her worries just then. "The hamper . . ." she gasped. "There's a snake in it. I heard a rattling—oh, thank God!" The last came in weak relief when he reached over and yanked the hamper from her hands, holding the lid tightly shut as he headed for the door.

"Get some clothes on!" he snapped over his shoulder. "I'll take care of this."

The hall door had sounded behind him before Lucie was able to take a deep breath and focus on her reflection in the mirror. She shook her head despairingly and then reached for a towel. It didn't matter, she told herself fiercely, mopping the tears from her cheeks. There were such things as priorities. Getting rid of a rattlesnake came at the top of her list. After that, arranging a plane ticket south was a close second.

Chapter
-6-

L ucie had just finished putting on a pair of pumps that matched her blue sun dress when a knock sounded on her bedroom door and Drew's voice came through the wood. "Lucie—are you okay?"

She went over to open it, brushing back her hair with still-shaky fingers before she turned the knob. "I'm fine," she announced, summoning a smile as she walked into the sitting room. "Sorry I was so long getting dressed."

The relief that showed in Drew's face when he saw her fully clothed showed that he was equally glad to ignore that embarrassing episode.

Her suspicions were confirmed by his quick change of subject. "You'd better have a drink. I told Paula to send up something to go with it."

Lucie felt her stomach lurch in protest at even the mention of food. "Really—I'm not hungry. Not a bit."

"See how you feel after a glass of something." He pushed back a paneled screen in the corner to reveal a small bar and rummaged in a compact refrigerator. "Champagne should do the trick."

Lucie shoved her hands in the pockets of her skirt

and walked reluctantly over to watch as he peeled foil from the neck of the bottle and eased out the cork. She waited until he'd handed her a hollow-stemmed glass full of the sparkling wine before she said, "There's no way you can ignore the subject much longer. Anybody would think you make a habit of keeping rattlesnakes in clothes hampers. Tell me, do you charge extra for them?"

"I know you're upset, but that's no reason to be ridiculous. Here—drink some champagne and stop talking like an idiot."

It was such a caustic putdown that Lucie was tempted to let fly with the champagne rather than stand there and meekly swallow it. Fortunately, her early deportment bore dividends; she managed to turn and walk over to the long windows rather than succumb to her impulse.

Drew watched her more carefully than she knew. She had such an expressive face that he had an amazingly accurate idea of what was going through her mind just then. He also knew that it wouldn't serve any purpose to follow his natural inclination and sympathize by taking her in his arms. In view of their embarrassing confrontation in the bath, she'd immediately think the worst.

He took a swallow of his champagne and perched on the arm of the couch to rest his aching leg. "If it's any consolation, that's the first rattlesnake we've ever had in the building. I can only hope to hell it's the last one."

The bleak undertone in his voice made Lucie turn slowly back to face him, her pique forgotten for the moment. "I don't understand. Why shouldn't it be? The odds against an accident like that must be stupendous."

Drew looked down at his glass and swirled its sparkling contents thoughtfully. "Accident being the operative word in this case. I'm pretty sure the snake was in that hamper because somebody took the trouble to plant him there."

"You mean the hamper didn't belong in the bathroom?"

He waved that aside. "The hamper did—but it was almost full of sheets and the maid never leaves clean linen stored in it. Obviously, it was put there to make it easy for the snake to escape over the top. That basket lid could be pushed up easily. You're just damned lucky that he hadn't made any overtures until then."

"Oh, don't!" Lucie shuddered visibly. "I shouldn't admit it, but snakes absolutely terrify me. I'd do better facing a grizzly—I think." The last two words were tacked on feebly.

"That's okay. You're in good company. Not many people choose to cuddle up to a rattler *or* a grizzly— even on rare occasions." Drew rubbed his forehead as if trying to think. "But why was it put there in the first place—that's the question."

"Well, there's always the outraged husband . . ."

". . . preceded by an accommodating wife." Drew shook his head. "Not guilty."

Lucie wanted to ask if Paula had any disappointed lovers on the landscape but she couldn't think of a diplomatic way of mentioning the subject. Fortunately, Drew went on before the silence lengthened.

"An unhappy employee would be another likely

prospect," he mused, "but it's been over a year since we've had to fire anybody."

"Not even a temporary employee?"

"There's a contingent of college help during the summer and most of them work for several seasons." He shook his head. "This isn't getting us anywhere."

"I was just thinking that maybe we're going about it wrong. It *is* your bathroom, but I was the one who was in it."

"I hadn't forgotten." For the first time, there was a thread of amusement in his voice.

Lucie hoped he didn't notice her heightened color as she went doggedly on. "It's like that crazy driver at the lodge in Jackson. You were the one who was hurt but only because you were busy shoving me out of the way."

"You think *you* were the intended target?" Drew's eyebrows came together across his tanned forehead as he considered it. "It's a possibility. Let's try Twenty Questions with you then. Any outraged wives gunning for you?"

"Not that I can think of. It doesn't even make sense. No woman in her right mind would be stuffing live rattlesnakes into a hamper."

"She'd be more apt to stuff an unfaithful husband in one," Drew agreed. "Okay, so we rule that out. Besides, Vito assures me he's unattached."

"What does he have to do with it?"

Drew got to his feet and went over to put his empty wine glass on the bar. "He's on the premises and ready to welcome you with open arms."

"Does he know I'm here?"

"I didn't tell him, but it wouldn't be hard for him to find out." Drew would have refilled her champagne glass, but when she shook her head, he replaced the bottle on the counter. "I don't know why we're wasting time discussing Perelli. Obviously, he's on the make, but it isn't a federal crime."

"Vito's been a perfect gentleman." Lucie's eyes flashed as she walked over to deposit her own glass on the bar counter. "Anybody would think that you're taking this big brother role seriously. Next, you'll be telling me that you're acting *in loco parentis* and checking the man's bank balance."

"It wouldn't be a bad idea if you're serious," Drew drawled, leaning on the counter. "I wouldn't expect anything too permanent from Mr. Perelli though— he isn't the type."

"Well, you'd be the first to recognize it," Lucie countered. "According to your father, you've avoided the sound of wedding bells with a vengeance for the past ten years. He told my mother that he'd hoped for grandchildren long before this.'

"When and *if* I get married, I'll make sure he's the first to know."

"You'd better check with Paula first—she might object." The words were out before Lucie was aware of it.

Drew was on his way toward the hall door but he swung around as quickly as his injured leg would permit. "What the hell does Paula have to do with it?"

"Well, I—assumed—that she'd be involved. She certainly looked as if she knew you very well. From the way she talked, it sounded like more than a business relationship." The expression on Drew's face should have stopped Lucie, but nervousness forced her on. "I'm sorry if I've—"

"Intimated that she's my mistress?" He moved toward her, taking his time about it. "Why apologize? It's always nice to know what people really think."

"I didn't say that . . ."

"I wonder what excuse you found for me that night in your cottage," he continued relentlessly. "With Paula on hand, there was no need for me to look for new talent."

"That's a rotten thing to say and completely un-called for." Lucie's chin firmed as he pulled up in front of her. "You have no right to go around insulting people all over the place."

He snorted. "Why is it that women keep harping on rights? My God, anybody would think that the Continental Congress wrote in a special section to give females that exclusive prerogative."

Lucie managed to look down her small straight nose at him and it wasn't easy, since he towered over her. "When I want a history lesson, I'll let you know. In the meantime, I suggest that you keep editorial comments about Vito or any other man in my life strictly to yourself."

"I suppose you're referring to that flake who phoned you at Jackson?"

Lucie ground her teeth together almost audibly. "That flake happens to be a very nice man."

"So nice that he collapsed like a sponge when I answered your phone at midnight."

"Why not? Just because you and . . ." she hesitated as she saw the dangerous glint in his eyes.

"Paula?" he prompted.

"It doesn't matter," she said hastily. "You're certainly old enough to do what you please."

"Consenting adults, eh? Well, since you've already written me off as a sex-fiend approaching senility," he reached out and caught her waist in an iron grip, "I might as well get some of the benefits."

"Don't be absurd," Lucie said, struggling to break his hold. "You've had all the benefits you're going to get today."

"Now what in the devil do you mean by that?"

Since she hadn't meant to mention that humiliating encounter by the bathroom hamper, her sense of frustration rose.

"*Will* you let go of me!" she said through gritted teeth, twisting to move out of range. "I don't have to explain anything to you, and the sooner you get it through that damned head of yours—the better it will be."

"And the sooner you learn that you can't go around shredding peoples' reputations the better off you'll be! Just because you've gotten the wrong idea . . ."

"Wrong idea! Hah!"

She broke off struggling long enough to stare defiantly at him and immediately found that was a mistake. Drew reached out and gripped the back of her head with one hand while sliding his other one around her waist to bring her up against him—hard. An instant later, his mouth captured hers in a ruthless and searching kiss.

Lucie stiffened as the kiss hardened and probed, trying to keep her lips tight against the sensuous onslaught. Drew made an angry noise in his throat and gave her an angry shake. "Dammit!" he murmured against her lips. "Don't tell me you need lessons in how to kiss a man!"

"Why, you—you conceited . . ."

Red-hot anger made her protest, and it was all the opportunity Drew needed. He kissed her again and this time her soft lips were parted, so she didn't have a chance to resist. Under Drew's expert persuasion, her last thought of resistance melted away, and when they gravitated to the soft cushions of the nearby couch a minute or so later, it was by mutual agreement.

After that, there was neither time nor inclination for discussion. Drew searched the sweetness of her mouth and his hands changed awareness to desire everywhere he touched her. When his lips finally rested against the hollow of her throat, Lucie instinctively cradled his head to her breast, smoothing his hair with gentle fingers.

A discreet knocking at the hall door did nothing to interrupt the idyll. It took a more forceful rapping before Drew straightened reluctantly, helping Lucie pull herself up from the soft cushions.

She managed to avoid his glance, feeling suddenly shy and breathless. Drew's reaction wasn't much better. His surface calm hadn't deserted him but his tone was rough as he focused on his watch and said, "Dammit—now what?" When he got up to answer the door, Lucie put out a detaining hand.

"Wait! There's some lipstick on your face," she said softly.

Wordlessly he pulled a clean handkerchief from his pocket and handed it to her. She took it and hastily rubbed a smudge from his jaw under his ear, even as she wondered how on earth it had gotten there. Surely she hadn't been so abandoned that—she broke off, blushing furiously, as she felt Drew's hand smooth the collar of her haltered sun dress.

"There," he said, calmly ignoring her discomfiture. "Nobody would ever know."

He walked quickly over then and opened the door. A room service waiter with a cart was on the other side of it, checking his list. "Mr. McLaren, did you order lunch?" he asked uncertainly. "Lunch for two?"

Drew nodded, motioning him in. "That's right, Carl. Sorry to keep you waiting. Bring it along." He glanced over to where Lucie stood, looking studiously out the big windows onto the patio below. "Miss Forsythe will tell you where she wants it served. I'll check in later, Lucie," and was gone before she could do more than turn to stare after him in dismay.

The waiter lingered until the door had closed behind Drew. Then he looked inquiringly at her.

"Oh, anywhere," Lucie said, trying to sound casual. "Perhaps by the window."

"I can put it on the balcony if you'd like, Miss Forsythe," he said, taking pity on her. "The weather's nice this time of day."

"Yes, of course. The balcony will be fine." Lucie managed to slide the window aside so he could wheel the trolley past her. It was on the tip of her tongue to say that eating was the last thing she wanted to do just then and for him to take it all away—but she lacked the necessary nerve. At least Drew had left her in peace, so she had a chance to sort things out. Although how she was going to face him the next time he appeared . . .

"Is there anything else, Miss Forsythe?"

She looked up to see the man waiting patiently by the door. "No—no, that's all," she said hastily. "Thank you very much."

"Then if you'll sign here, please. That's fine, thanks." The man gave her a cheerful smile and closed the door behind him.

Lucie went over to sink on the couch and put her palms up to cool her hot cheeks as she leaned back against the cushions. Then she remembered what had happened there just a few minutes before. She said, "Oh, Lord," and stood up again. Which was ridiculous, she told herself. A woman didn't turn into a dithering idiot because a man kissed her a time or two.

Kissed her a time or two. Now that was the understatement of the year. Like calling a tidal wave a marine disturbance or labeling an avalanche as a slight shift in the earth's surface.

One minute she and Drew had been snarling at each other and the next—the next was something she'd never experienced. It was like suddenly viewing her surroundings through a diffused lens. There were no sharp edges—just softness and muted colors and an intensity of newfound desire that didn't bear examining.

Lucie bit her lip and walked over to the balcony, reaching down to pour a cup of coffee. Not that she wanted it, she told herself. Just anything to stop thinking about her reactions to what had happened. Only reaction didn't tell the whole story either, she thought despairingly. Change it to surrender. It was just a good thing the room service waiter had appeared when he did.

As if on cue, there came another knocking from the hall. Lucie put down the coffee cup, moving over to the closed door to ask hesitantly, "Who is it?"

"Paula—Paula Bennett, remember? Lucie, are you all right in there?"

Lucie took a deep breath, resting her forehead for an instant against the cool wood before she reached for the doorknob. Just how much, she wondered, did Paula know about what had happened? And how did she happen to appear so promptly on the scene.

The blonde secretary settled both questions as soon as Lucie opened the door. "I heard about that horrible snake," she said in her forthright manner, walking past Lucie into the sitting room. "You poor soul! I was on my way up to commiserate with you when I met Drew in the hall just now, and he said you might like company for lunch. Help dull the blow—so to speak. Ummm—roast beef sandwiches," she said from the balcony where she'd gone to inspect the tray of food. "I hoped somebody might invite me to share the calories when I ordered this earlier." She turned to smile unabashed at Lucie. "There's enough for two, honest."

Lucie smiled thoughtfully back and waved her to a

chair by the table. Considering what had just taken place, Drew's decision to send his private secretary in was either a touch of madness or he was showing Lucie that he had no intention of permanently changing his ways—despite momentary lapses. And yet it was impossible for her to dislike the attractive widow who was calmly pouring herself a cup of coffee and making herself at home.

Paula looked up, slightly amused by Lucie's discreet appraisal. "You'd better have some food," the older woman said, gesturing toward a chair by the wrought iron balcony railing. "Sit over there where there's the most breeze. It takes a while to get used to the altitude here. To say nothing of a rattlesnake on the premises." Paula took a sip of coffee and made a satisfied murmur. "Maybe Walter will be able to figure it out. I can't wait to tell him."

Lucie sat down and leaned forward to rest her elbows on the table, holding her coffee cup between her palms. "Who's Walter? The manager?"

Paula's eyes crinkled with laughter. "Not really. He's a business associate of Drew's—sort of a financial advisor to the family and a tax lawyer."

"Does he have an office here?"

"Uh-huh," Paula managed through a bite of sandwich, "but he's in Chicago right now on a business trip. Drew was with him until he came west to meet you." She pushed the plate of sandwiches toward Lucie. "Better have one. Drew will want a report when I get back to work."

Lucie shook her head, refusing to follow orders by remote control. If Drew felt any real concern about her well-being, he could have stuck around and tended to it personally. "I'm not hungry. How was your flight back?"

"Uneventful. Drew had to be talked into seeing the doctor when we got into Flagstaff. Fortunately, his leg was healing properly and he should be walking normally by the time your folks get back. We're all anxious to meet your mother," Paula said.

Lucie managed to murmur noncommittally, wondering what her mother would think if she learned of Paula's and Drew's close relationship.

Paula dusted her fingers on a napkin and sighed with satisfaction as she leaned back in her chair to finish her coffee. "All of us who live here feel like members of a big family. Some of our guests have been coming back for years. And now that Drew and his father have decided to restore the old ghost town, there should be a tremendous upsurge in the daily visitors."

Lucie was glad that Paula'd gone on to a safer topic than family relationships. It wasn't a term that Lucie even wanted to think about just then—since Drew's actions and her own behavior hardly belonged in that category.

"Are you feeling all right?" Paula straightened, surveying her closely.

"Of course. Why?"

"The way you looked just then, I thought you were in pain."

"The sun's getting to me," Lucie prevaricated. "I'll move my chair into the shade. Where is this ghost town you mentioned? Can I see it before I leave?"

"Heavens, yes. It's just about four or five miles beyond the stables," Paula said, waving in that general direction. "Anybody can show you the way, but don't try to hike unless the sun's down. It would be easier to drive or go on horseback."

Lucie shook her head, "That's what you think. I'll take my chances on two feet. Didn't you hear about my troubles with Marmaduke?"

"Who's Marmaduke?"

"A passing acquaintance," Lucie said, happy that the mishaps of her trail ride had been allowed to die a natural death rather than amuse Paula on the flight south.

"He didn't follow you down here, did he?"

"I should think it most unlikely," Lucie said, straight-faced. "Why?"

"Drew looked pretty upset when I met him in the hall just now. I thought maybe you'd been arguing about something or someone." Paula paused expectantly but when Lucie didn't respond, she persisted. "Am I right?"

"Sort of. To be honest, I can't remember what started it off."

Fortunately, Paula didn't see anything strange in her spiritless response. "Drew has a short fuse—but then I've found it's better not to argue with any man. Why bother? A woman can usually win in other ways."

"You make it sound like a constant competition."

"Ever since Eve." Paula pushed back her chair. "And I don't care what the feminists say—it always will be. Now I have to get back to the office or I'll be working a swing shift. What are you going to do for the rest of the day?"

"I hadn't thought," Lucie stalled, knowing very well that she was going to stay out of Drew's way until she could finalize her arrangements to go on down to Phoenix. "Probably explore the grounds or something."

"I can arrange for a car if you'd like to go into the Park and peer over the edge of the Grand Canyon. There's nothing that can match it for sheer magnitude."

"I know. Actually I've already seen it, but maybe I can take another quick look before I leave."

"Vito might be happy to act as chauffeur." Paula lingered by the hall door. "He's been pestering me to find out when you were coming. Has he called you yet?"

"No. To be honest, I'd forgotten that he was staying here."

Paula's wide smile flashed. "Well, don't tell Vito that. He's convinced that he has a quail ready for plucking."

"What a thing to say! I don't know how he got that idea."

"Vito Perelli was born with that one thought in mind," Paula drawled, "and he'll still be working on it when they lower him in a pine box. Give any man a profile and he feels duty-bound to live up to it. I'm glad that Walter thinks a mirror is strictly for shaving or combing his hair." Seeing Lucie's puzzled expression, she went on blithely as she opened the door. "I told you about Walter earlier. He's my fiancé."

"Your what?" It was an incredulous whisper.

"My fiancé. What's so strange about that?"

"Nothing—except that I thought—I—" Lucie found herself stammering. "Somehow I presumed that you and Drew . . ."

Paula's wide smile flashed. "Honey—you didn't! Why, Drew's going to be Walter's best man. He and his father are giving us a South Seas honeymoon as their wedding present. Isn't that wonderful?"

Lucie tried desperately to assimilate this latest bombshell. If what Paula said was true, then Drew was innocent as well.

Paula watched the play of emotion over the other's face and reached out to pat her arm comfortingly. "Don't worry. It'll all work out. Most of us act like halfwits at one time or another."

"I could teach a course on it. Do you suppose it would do any good if I apologized?"

"To Drew?" Paula chuckled. "If I know that man, he'll get a pound of flesh as well. Figuratively speaking, of course. Oh, dear, that sounds even worse." She went back to open the hall door. "Go take a dip in the pool and practice your wiles on Vito this afternoon. By dinnertime, you'll have all the right words down pat."

"What happens then? I mean—do I eat up here or in the dining room?" Lucie tried to think what she'd been told.

"You'll be at the family table downstairs. Drew will show you. He usually eats around seven. If I hear anything different, I'll give you a jingle this afternoon. Thanks for the sandwich." Paula waggled her fingers, winked, and closed the door.

Her cheerful manner was contagious. Or perhaps learning the truth of Paula's engagement was responsible for Lucie's brand-new feeling that life was good. Of course, she still had to apologize to Drew and he might read her the riot act. On the other hand, he hadn't acted like a man who was completely immune to feminine persuasion the last time she'd seen him.

She took a deep breath and came back to normal. What she needed was to get out and explore the premises rather than sit around like some soggy character in a soap opera.

She pulled a nubby shirt-jacket from the top of her suitcase and put it on, tucking a key to the suite in her pocket afterward. The shoes she had on were comfortable, good for walking or even cycling to the ghost town. She'd take a dip in the pool before dinner. From then on, she'd have to play it by ear.

Unfortunately, things didn't work out quite as Lucie intended. She had no sooner gone through the front door of the hotel, intent on finding the cycle shop, than she saw Vito bending over an open car window holding a discussion with the man behind the wheel. It was too late for her to duck back in the hotel again without attracting his attention, so she averted her head and moved quickly down the walk edging the drive.

"Lucie!" Vito's voice boomed out even before she got abreast of the car and she pulled up, trying to look surprised.

"Vito! How nice to see you. But you're busy—" She gestured toward the man in the car who was staring at her. "I'll talk to you later."

"No, no," Vito insisted. "We're finished. My friend here is already late." He glanced down at the driver who was reaching for the ignition switch. "Keep in touch."

The man nodded, gave Lucie another cursory glance, and drove off.

"Now—all my work is done. There is nothing to interrupt us . . ." Vito broke off as he noticed her slight frown. "What's the matter?"

"Nothing important. I just remembered something," Lucie replied, encountering his suspicious glance. "It doesn't matter. I'll take care of it later." That was an out and out lie, but more diplomatic than saying, "I've seen that man somewhere before. Who in the dickens is he?"

"Women!" Vito's smug comment showed what he thought of feminine mentality. "Always going back to check and see if the stove is off."

"Or the iron is on. Let's hope I don't burn the hotel down this time," she added. "I'm sure I turned it off." It was a safe conclusion since her travel iron hadn't been taken out of the suitcase. "I was on my way to rent a bicycle and look at McLaren's ghost town."

"I'm surprised that Drew isn't giving you a personal tour. Does he know you're here?"

"Oh, yes," which was an understatement if she'd ever made one, "but he's busy. Besides, I don't need a guide."

"Well, you have one," Vito said, taking her hand in

a firm clasp. "A car, too. Bicycles aren't my thing. Now, I wouldn't object to a nice horseback ride—"

"I would," Lucie said drily. "Anyhow, neither of us is dressed for it. Especially you." She let her glance go swiftly over the beige slacks and sport shirt which complemented his tanned skin.

He shrugged, but it was easy to see that he was flattered by her remark. "We'll take my car and come back afterward and have a cool drink by the pool."

"That doesn't sound very organic or outdoorish."

"If you want to go back to nature, we'll walk the rim trail along the Canyon tomorrow." He was leading her to his sleek sports car which was parked down at the end of the drive as he spoke. "It should be in the morning, before it gets too hot."

She waited for him to open the car door and then sat in a red leather bucket seat. "You sound as if you'd stayed around here lots of times. What's the attraction?"

"It's hard to say. One resort hotel's pretty much like another but the McLaren's run an efficient operation here. The food's good—so's the service. I'm not keen on this ghost town development, though. I told Drew that he was going to lose a lot of his repeat guests. Nobody wants to have the landscape cluttered with transient traffic."

"You may have a point there." Lucie was admiring the competent way Vito handled the car as he accelerated out of the driveway and onto a two-lane road which led past the attractive outbuildings in back of the hotel. Beyond the good-sized corral, he increased speed as they drove through rugged plateau land

where the limestone soil was sparsely covered with
wild grasses and some straggly ponderosa pines.
Rocks were the most plentiful commodity in the landscape, and a little farther beyond, Lucie wasn't surprised when they approached two men constructing a
wall of native stone at the apparent outskirts of a
deserted mining town. The stonemasons looked
startled but not upset when Vito drove around a crude
barricade of oil drums at the entrance, heading up the
gentle hillside toward what had once been the center
of town.

The years had shown little mercy and most of the
buildings had only partial stone fronts left of their
original one-story frames. On some of them, door and
window casements survived, but all of the wooden
roofs had disappeared.

"That was the post office," Vito said, gesturing as
he pulled up in front of an adobe facade which still
had a partial wooden porch attached. "The barber
shop was down that way along with the local bawdy
house and bar."

"All it needs is Marshal Dillon coming around the
corner." Lucie stared around her, fascinated. "What
were they mining for here? Gold? Silver?"

"Gold. At least that's what Drew told me. It was
one of the few mines in this part of the country to tap
an underground vein. He's planned a museum to show
people how the place looked in about 1900 when it
was in full swing."

"It sounds like a tremendous project," she said. She
pointed to a diamond-shaped, waist-high rock struc-
ture not far ahead of them that looked about twenty

feet to a side. "What on earth's that? The Druids didn't spend any time here, did they?"

"Hardly. That's a water reservoir. Nonfunctioning, of course. The McLarens put in some wood flooring to be on the safe side." Vito reached over to shift gears. "Have you seen enough?"

"I guess so. Unless you want to get out and poke around," she offered hopefully.

"There's no point in ending up all hot and dusty. Damned if I can understand Drew's enthusiasm to restore this place. How many people are going to want to waste time exploring relics?"

"Evidently enough. It looks as if they're planning to fence the premises," she said, gesturing toward the two men constructing the walled entrance by the highway turnoff, as Vito drove back down the hill a minute later. "That makes sense—I suppose they'll need security forces as well, when they have the place put back together. It's a big investment."

Vito shrugged, accelerating so that a cloud of dust rose behind them when they drove back on the main road.

"Oh, those poor men," Lucie said, turning to peer through the back window.

"They're getting paid. Let them complain to Drew," Vito said callously. "Eating dust is one of the problems in this part of the state. There's usually a wind to guarantee it."

"It's beautiful today—" she began, only to have him cut her off.

". . . that's why I suggested a swim. Might as well take advantage of the weather. Although they do put up glass windbreaks around the patio pool if they need them," Vito admitted. "I hope you brought a suit with you. The natives frown on skinny-dipping in the afternoon."

"I should think so," Lucie said. "That pool's a little public any time of the day."

Vito turned with a flashing grin. "Want to give it a try after midnight?"

Lucie's grip tightened on the edge of her seat as they narrowly missed a car coming the opposite way. "At this rate, we won't live that long."

"Sorry." He gave his attention to the road once again. "You had me all excited there."

"I didn't mean to. You'll have to find somebody else for your nighttime outings. Skinny-dipping doesn't fit my newfound family image."

"And besides—you aren't really tempted," he announced. "Okay, we'll follow the original plans. Even big brother Drew couldn't object to those." He pulled into the hotel drive a few minutes later and parked close to the door, ignoring the loading zone signs.

Lucie lingered after he'd joined her on the curb. "I like your car. You didn't have it with you in Wyoming, did you?"

"No—a friend delivered it here. It makes it easier to take care of my business." As they reached the lodge doors, he looked at his watch. "Meet you by the pool in a half hour?"

She nodded. "That's about right."

"Okay. Bring a wrap so we don't have to hurry. Once the sun gets low, there's a real drop in the temperature at this altitude."

Lucie discovered that he knew what he was talking about. Even though the pool was heated, they weren't tempted to linger in the water after their swim. The wind that Vito had mentioned earlier started as a gentle breeze but an insistent one.

"You were right about the temperature," she said, tightening the belt of her terry coverup and trying to peer up at the sky around the top of their umbrella table near the poolside. "Two hours ago, it felt like summer and now I'm sorry that I didn't pack some thermal underwear."

"Better bring a sweater for our Canyon excursion tomorrow morning, too," Vito said. Even though the sun was almost down, he was still only wearing an unbuttoned cotton shirt over his damp swim trunks.

Lucie suspected that he didn't want to hide the pelt of dark hair on his broad chest. Then, feeling guilty at such an uncharitable thought, she said, "Are you sure that you have time to take me sightseeing tomorrow? It can't be much fun for you going around to familiar places."

"Lucie, *cara*—I'm just sorry that I have to wait until then." His instant response was reassuring. So was the smoldering look he directed across the table at her. "It's a shame that I'm tied up for dinner. Sure you won't change your mind about a late night swim?"

She laughed softly, presenting a picture of lissome grace as she pushed back in her chair. "Not a chance. Only a polar bear would be tempted in this weather."

"All right, then." He stood up as she did. "We'll meet tomorrow about nine. I'll make sure that I finish my business tonight so we can take time for lunch on

our excursion. The dining room at El Tovar Lodge
overlooks the Canyon—you'll enjoy it."

"Thanks, it sounds very nice." Privately Lucie was
wondering how she could avoid any other invitations
without offending him. It would be nice if Drew
materialized to offer an excuse, she thought wryly, instead of doing his disappearing act. Perhaps he'd show
up at dinner and they'd be able to sort things out for
the rest of her time at the resort. In the meantime, it
was kind of Vito to be so flattering in his attention. As
a result of her soul-searching, her tone was warmer
than usual and she put out an impulsive hand as they
lingered by the table. "Vito—you've been awfully
nice. I enjoyed the ride and the swim."

Vito's eyes darkened and he pulled her close, letting
her feel his strength. "I could think of better places to
say goodby—even for a little while."

Before she could speak, he leaned down and kissed
her. There wasn't any gentleness in his action, nor was
there any hesitation. When he raised his head, he
stared at her surprised face, then gripped her wrist for
an instant before releasing it. "Don't forget me, *cara*.
We'll talk more tomorrow."

"Yes—yes, of course." Lucie was annoyed to feel
the sudden warmth in her cheeks and knew that Vito
hadn't missed it either. No wonder he was looking at
her with such an air of satisfaction.

As she headed for the stairs, she was ruefully shaking her head. Vito apparently made a lifetime project
of kissing women. The only thing that spoiled the general effect was the certain knowledge that he knew
how accomplished he was at the task. Lucie could

have told him that his technique wasn't quite as good as he thought, but even so, it had been a memorable afternoon. If her luck held, the night might be even better.

Chapter

– 7 –

When Lucie unlocked the door to her suite, she wasn't really surprised to find the sitting room still deserted. She went into her bedroom and got out of her swimsuit, changing to a silky apricot print which had a piped neckline and pleated skirt that did nice things for her figure. After she'd applied lipstick of the same apricot shade, she checked her appearance in the full-length mirror on the bedroom door. If she'd looked woebegone the last time Drew had seen her— the effect was long gone. Inside she might be still feeling butterflies at meeting him again, but the outside facade was glossy.

She looked at her wristwatch as she went back into the sitting room and then wandered aimlessly around the suite. He should have appeared by now, she thought, and frowned as she stared down onto the patio. Beyond the outer walls, she could see headlights of an occasional car moving along the road she'd traveled with Vito earlier in the day. Her expression was thoughtful as she recalled the luxury of his expensive sports car. His business must be lucrative indeed to warrant such extravagance. The man he'd been talking to at the hotel entrance was driving a late model car as well, and Lucie wondered idly if he was a business associate. It was strange how familiar he'd looked. If she thought about it tomorrow, she'd ask Vito if he worked in San Francisco.

The phone rang sharply at that moment. Drew, she thought with an unsteady breath, and hurried over to lift the receiver. "Hullo."

"Lucie? You must be starving by now," Paula spoke in her usual crisp way. "How about coming down to join me for dinner."

"I'd like to, but Drew said something about getting together."

"I know." There was an undertone of impatience in the other's voice. "Unfortunately, he isn't here. He asked me to let you know."

"Isn't here?" Lucie fastened on the important words. "What do you mean?"

"Just that. He was called to a meeting in Phoenix this afternoon. Look, I'll tell you all about it over dinner. See you in the dining room?"

"Yes, of course." Lucie tried not to show her disappointment. "I'll be there in five minutes."

When she joined Paula in the attractive eating place a little later, she discovered that they were to be the only occupants of the "family table" by the windows.

Paula, dressed in an emerald shirtwaist of a gauzy material, smiled a welcome as Lucie was seated and given a menu. "Will you have a cocktail?" the secretary asked, while the waiter hovered.

"No, thanks. But don't let me stop you."

Paula shook her head. "I'm still working. Give us a few minutes, Rudy—we'll order then."

"Right, Mrs. Bennett."

She turned back to Lucie and found that she was looking around, obviously more intrigued by her surroundings than by the prospect of food. "It's nicely done, isn't it?" Paula said in a tone of satisfaction.

Lucie nodded. Wall murals of southwest scenes and a carpet of Indian symbols augmented the room's attractive atmosphere. Copper was the dominant color, repeated in the leather chairs, wall sconces, and chandelier. Wide windows along one wall revealed the illuminated gardens of the inner patio.

"The food's marvelous, too," Paula said when she saw she had Lucie's attention again. "Drew and his father make sure of that. Your mother will be lucky if she doesn't gain ten pounds in the first month."

"I'll have to warn her." Lucie opened the big menu and kept her glance on the printed contents as she asked casually, "You said you'd explain about Drew. What kind of meeting is he attending?"

"I can't contribute much. This is one time when he didn't give me many details." Paula pushed her own menu aside and leaned on her elbows. "Drew isn't a man to bare his soul at any time, but I've never known him to be quite this close-mouthed. He was on the phone to Phoenix and the next thing I knew—he was on his way out of the office, saying he had an unexpected meeting."

"I see."

"Well, I'm darned if I do," Paula grumbled good-naturedly. She broke off as a waiter came to take their order and then resumed when the man picked up their menus and started toward the kitchen. "I've been stalling people who wanted to get in touch with Drew all afternoon. He didn't even say whether he'd be back tonight or tomorrow." She reached out to break a cracker and nibbled on a piece of it. "He simply got in his car and left."

Lucie didn't say anything until she'd been served with a cup of vichyssoise resting in a bowl of chipped ice. "Did he leave any message for me?"

"Just that I was to make sure you were taken care of for dinner. Oh, there was one other thing . . ." Paula touched her napkin to her lips. "He wants you to stick close to the hotel. Not wander around much until he gets back."

Lucie's spoon halted in midair. "Why?"

"What do you mean?" Paula asked, her tone non-committal.

"You know. Why should I stick close?" Lucie sounded rebellious. "Is this house arrest or just Drew's usual way of doing things?"

"Now don't get upset—"

"I'm not upset—I'm furious." Lucie started to push her vichyssoise away and then changed her mind.

Paula looked on approvingly. "That's the girl. No man is worth missing dinner for. Probably Drew just wanted to make sure that you didn't scoot off to Phoenix or Scottsdale before he could get back. I won't tell anyone if you want to do some local sightseeing tomorrow—like checking out the Canyon. As a matter of fact, you can borrow my car."

"That's kind of you but it isn't necessary. I've already made plans."

"Oh?" Paula's eyebrows climbed. "Let me guess—Vito's been hard at work."

"He's offered to take me hiking along a rim nature trail in the morning," Lucie said, surprised to find herself on the defensive. "I thought it was nice of him."

"Vito isn't the type to be 'nice.' He hasn't made a spontaneous gesture since he left the womb. You're part of a long-range plan or I miss my guess."

"That's absurd." Lucie laughed at Paula's suspicions despite herself. "Anyhow, I'm not about to co-operate. All I have in mind is a nice walk along the rim trail and maybe lunch at El Tovar later."

"I shouldn't think that Drew could raise any objection to that itinerary," Paula said, starting on the green salad which had just been placed in front of her.

"That's nice." Lucie made no effort to hide the sarcasm in her voice. "Sorry, Paula, but even the people I work for don't go around issuing ultimatums. I'm surprised that Drew has any employees."

"He doesn't usually act this way—" The words were out before Paula knew it and she put her hand up to her forehead in a theatrical gesture. "So much for diplomacy."

Lucie ignored that. "Maybe it's because I'm a shirttail relative. If that's the case, though, I think he'd be shoving me out the front door."

"He'll probably tell us all as soon as he comes back. In the meantime, I wouldn't worry about your status. Drew didn't look like an irate hotelkeeper when I met him in the hall this afternoon." Paula waved a salad fork to emphasize her point. "He looked like a man who was walking around in a fog—or maybe it was a cloud with pearl linings."

"Coming face to face with a rattlesnake leaves most anybody in shock," Lucie countered, trying to pass it off. "I didn't breathe normally for an hour afterward."

"Yes, but the gardener who took care of the rattler said Drew wasn't the least bit upset—" Paula broke off. "It doesn't matter. I imagine Vito was flabbergasted when he heard about it."

"I don't believe I told him," Lucie said, trying to remember. "We drove out to the ghost town and he was busy talking about it. Canyon Hill should be fascinating when it's restored."

"I agree. Drew and his father have wanted to do it for a long time, but it hasn't been easy. They've had to confer with the state historical society and all kinds of environmental groups."

"From the way Vito talked, it won't be long now. He's just afraid that it'll end up with a carnival atmosphere," Lucie added apologetically. "Actually, he wasn't enthusiastic."

"As if he was an expert," Paula said scornfully. "Drew knows better than to be discouraged by comments like that."

"I didn't agree either, but there was no point in getting in a slanging match with Vito."

"Especially when it doesn't matter. The restoration should start officially sometime this week. Maybe Drew's finalizing the contracts right now. Although I think he could have told me." Paula smiled ruefully. "A man's secretary is always the last to know."

Paula's comment was the only comforting thing that Lucie took to bed with her that night. She spent the last part of the evening watching television in lonesome splendor in her bedroom, unconsciously hoping for the phone to ring. It remained stubbornly silent and she went to bed, feeling thoroughly out of sorts with the world.

Thin rays of sunlight edged the curtains at her bedroom window the next morning when her alarm went off. After Lucie shut off the buzzer, she stretched lazily and contemplated the day ahead without enthusiasm. It was all very well to keep telling herself that Vito was as handsome as a Greek god and that hundreds of women would be charmed to spend the day with him, but her sales talk was falling short. All because the far less perfect profile of a man named Drew McLaren managed to cloud her every waking thought. Plus a few of her dreams, Lucie acknowledged, remembering her restless night.

She got out of bed then and went over to check the weather on the patio before heading for the shower. The sun was shining in a cloudless sky, but there was already a breeze rustling the limbs of the pine tree by her balcony. Slacks and sweater weather, she decided. At least until midday.

She ate breakfast in the resort coffee shop, determined to pay her own way as much as possible. After she went back to the suite and collected a scarf and her shoulder bag, it was time to meet Vito in the lobby.

He was just coming through the door as she reached the ground floor. Seeing his expression brighten, she felt a twinge of guilt at her reluctance to keep the date.

"*Cara*, you look marvelous this morning," he said, catching her by the hands and letting his gaze wander over her like a man drinking his fill. "Absolutely marvelous."

Lucie's first reaction was that he had either been drinking or needed glasses. Her green slacks and blouse with its scarf collar fitted well but were hardly whistlebait. Neither was the matching belted jacket. She bit her lip to hide her amusement. "Thank you, Vito. That's kind of you—so early in the morning, too!"

He had taken her elbow to steer her toward the door but pulled up at her remark. "Now what do you mean by that?"

"Nothing vital. It's just that most men wouldn't be so"— she searched for the word that would satisfy him—"so considerate."

"If a woman is beautiful—I tell her. No matter what the hour."

Lucie's sense of humor almost was her undoing then as she visualized all of the decidedly inconvenient times that Vito could choose to pay his compliments.

"And you, *cura*, are very beautiful." Vito's voice reverberated through the lobby, causing more than one head to crane in their direction. "Especially this morning."

Lucie started for the entrance, without any more discussion. It was better than flatly announcing she didn't believe a word of it. Her restless night had taken its toll, which meant Vito's compliments were as phony as the eyelashes on an overweight redhead walking across the lobby. Lucie waited long enough for Vito to appreciate the woman's mincing gait before asking, "Is your car parked in the drive?"

He brought his attention back with an effort. "Yes, of course. But have you had breakfast? We could stop for another cup of coffee. After all, the Canyon won't run away."

"Let's have it later at one of the cafeterias in Grand Canyon Village," she said, determined to get out of the lobby before he could attract any more attention.

"Whatever you say," Vito said, shrugging as they went through the door. "It might be better. Safer, too."

She hesitated, looking across at him. "In what way?"

"I'd rather have you to myself. If we stay around here, Drew will materialize. It never fails. Every time I meet a beautiful woman at this hotel . . ." Vito's comment trailed off as he realized what he'd said.

"Then we'd better get going," Lucie replied, charitably overlooking his gaffe. "Drew isn't the type to spend his mornings on a nature walk at the Canyon rim, so you should be safe."

Vito bestowed a sardonic look as he bent to open the car door for her. He closed it and went around to get behind the wheel. "I don't make a habit of it, either. You aren't the type of woman who'd go along with other invitations. I noticed that yesterday. That's why I suggested drinks by the pool instead of in my room. Or yours."

Lucie didn't answer. Her cheeks were more flushed

than usual because she was remembering the scene that had transpired with Drew in her sitting room the day before. Had Vito even suspected it, he wouldn't have been so conservative in his maneuvering.

Vito couldn't have known the way her thoughts were going, but his next words showed that there was nothing wrong with his eyesight. "Why are you blushing, *cara*? Ah—I've embarrassed you because of my frank approach. No—don't interrupt." He waved her to silence. "It's because I don't have much time for preliminary skirmishing. I can't stay around here long when my business is finished. But that doesn't mean that our friendship can't continue."

She cut in before he could go any further. "Of course not, Vito. I'll look forward to your calling me in San Francisco when I get back to work. Surely your business brings you up there?" She went on to explain, "San Francisco is a headquarters for imports, isn't it?"

"Oh, that." His expression cleared. "Imports are just a sideline for me. I have more important projects."

"I'm impressed. No, I mean it," she insisted when his thick eyebrows rose. "And grateful, too—that you'd take a morning off to go sightseeing."

"It's a pleasure, *cara*." He reached out to pat her hand which happened to be resting on her thigh.

Lucie pulled her fingers away quickly on the pretense of searching for a handkerchief in her purse and relaxed visibly when he put his hand back on the steering wheel.

Her gaze was ostensibly on the steadily increasing traffic on the road leading into the Grand Canyon National Park, but she was trying to think of something to keep Vito from attempting any more passes— disguised or otherwise. Nervously she mentioned the first thing that came into her head. "I meant to ask if you'd finished your business with the man in the car yesterday."

Vito cut sharply in front of the car he was passing, receiving an indignant blast of the other's horn in protest. "What man are you talking about?" he wanted to know.

"Oh!" Lucie, who had wondered if they'd make it, let out her breath sharply. "He was awfully mad."

"Now you aren't making sense. *Who* was mad? None of my friends . . ."

"No, I meant that driver in the car behind us." She rubbed her forehead distractedly. "Before that, I was talking about the man at the hotel yesterday. You said he was a business associate."

"*Cara*, I think you should have had your coffee." Vito's manner was urbane again. "What about that man?"

"Well, nothing," Lucie stammered. "It sounds silly, I know—but I thought I recognized him. He reminded me of a customer I had last spring," she said, suddenly remembering.

"Was there something special about this customer of yours?"

"Not really. I might have him confused with someone else. Why, we're at the park gates already," she said quickly as he had to slow and get in line with the other cars to pay the park entrance fee and receive a permit. "It's crowded for so early in the morning."

Vito inched the car along in line. "This park is always crowded. You'll be surprised at the number of foreigners visiting. Grand Canyon is one of the places they all want to see."

By then, they had drawn abreast of the park entrance booth and Vito had his money ready. A ranger thanked him and handed Lucie a brochure and map of the facilities, announcing that the staff of the Visitor's Center would be glad to answer any questions, before waving them on.

Lucie raised her window as Vito accelerated, following a sign for the West Rim Drive. "If you're serious about the Nature Walk, I suppose we'd better park at the Visitors's Center," he said. "Then we can go to Mather Point or down toward the hotel and lodges."

"That sounds good," Lucie agreed, caught up in the excitement of the scene. Even a repeat visit to one of the seven Natural Wonders of the World made her sit on the edge of the car seat. "Aren't we lucky that the weather is so good?"

"The breeze isn't going away," Vito said, gesturing toward the piñon juniper bending under it at the roadside. "We'll end up with dirt in our faces, instead of fresh air."

"I don't care." Lucie lowered her window again. "It smells marvelous. Even the dirt is pine-scented around here."

"Plus carbon monoxide from that damned truck," Vito grunted, nodding toward the camper in front of them.

"You're a cynic. I really envy people their first

glimpse of the Canyon. After all these miles of stunted pine trees and rocky landscape, suddenly the most awe-inspiring sight in the world is spread out in front of you." Lucie's expression was enraptured as she went on. "It's strange how no picture or movie does it justice. You have to see it in person." She grimaced apologetically then. "The Chamber of Commerce would love me."

"That's okay." He hesitated as they reached a fork in the road. "Let's go straight to the parking lot by the Visitors' Center and get rid of the car. There's no point in joining the mobs at Mather Point now."

"All right." Lucie had been anticipating at least a quick look at the popular viewpoint but subsided. After all, she told herself, few men waxed rhapsodic over scenery, no matter how spectacular.

Vito uttered some caustic comments about the traffic thronging the roads and cyclists who took more than their share of the pavement, but it wasn't long before they reached the modern Visitors' Center and parked in the lot beside it.

When they got out of the car, Vito reached back to retrieve a 35mm camera in a case and hung the strap 'round his neck. Lucie, who was watching, started to chuckle. He frowned at her across the hood of the car. "Something amuses you?" he asked defensively.

"I'm sorry." She bit her lip, unable to confess that it was like seeing Apollo step down from his pedestal and pull an Instamatic from his toga. "Everybody is a camera fiend these days," she said lightly. "I hope you'll send me one or two prints if you get something good. I left my camera at home."

Vito's expression cleared and he waved an expansive hand. "I'm not expecting much on the rim walk—there are too many people. If we can get by ourselves, there's a better chance for a decent picture." He locked the car and shoved the key in the pocket of his slacks. Even for such a casual outing, he was wearing gabardine trousers and a white terry cloth jac-shirt which looked custom-made. Lucie smiled again as she trailed him across the crowded parking area, wondering irreverently if his pajama trousers had knife pleats?

Fortunately, she'd smothered her amusement when he pulled up in front of the building, gesturing disdainfully toward the throngs of people inside. "There's no need to waste time here, is there?" he asked.

"I suppose not," she said uncertainly. "Unless we could find out when the rangers have scheduled the next walk."

A woman standing nearby overheard her. "You're in luck," she said. "A group just left. You can still catch up with them. See—they're down there on the path toward the amphitheater." She gestured toward a cluster of people who were strolling behind a girl wearing the green uniform of a Park Ranger.

"Oh, marvelous." Lucie smiled her thanks. "C'mon, Vito—let's hurry."

"But Lucie—" He had to lengthen his stride to keep up with her as she started down the wide dirt track. "There's no need for us to join a group, for God's sake. I thought we were going to be on our own."

"Please, Vito—" She put an appealing hand on his

arm. "Let's join the group for a while. Afterward, there's time to go on down the rim walk by ourselves."

"Oh, all right." Vito didn't look happy but he accompanied her without any more comments. They caught up with the group listening to the attractive girl ranger who was standing beside a ponderosa pine with a walkie-talkie in her hand.

"You'll find these all along the canyon rim," the girl was saying. "The bark turns to an orange color when the tree is between three to four hundred years old."

"That one doesn't look so good right now," Vito put in, *sotto voce*. When Lucie ignored him, he sighed and started fiddling with his camera case.

"If you come close to the tree," the ranger continued, unaware that she'd lost one member of her audience, "you'll notice a definite vanilla smell in the sap. The ants around here love the ooze. Now—follow me, please."

Lucie moved with the others to a group of low plants alongside the path, leaving Vito photographing the sky through the branches of the pine tree. He tired of that after a minute or two and came to join them.

"This is called the spiny Desert Phlox," the ranger lectured. "Indians in this area used to grind it and place it on their gums to deaden the pain of a toothache. Once that was accomplished, they'd harden pitch from the piñon pine tree and use it to fill the cavity. Now, this tree," she pointed to one just ahead of them, "is the Utah juniper. The holes in the trunk are made by yellow-bellied sapsuckers who consume sap and insects they find there. You'll also find mistletoe up in the branches. The roots of the juniper were used by the Indians to make a red dye." She patted the tree trunk almost affectionately. "Quite a going concern. Not like the sagebrush next to it," she said, leading the group on down the path.

"How much more of this is there?" Vito hissed in Lucie's ear.

"I'd like to hear this part," she replied, wishing he'd at least try to pay attention. "It's really fascinating to learn the background."

"The official name for sagebrush is *Artemisia tridentata*," the ranger said, straightening her "Smokey Bear" hat so that it rested squarely atop her blonde hair. "Artemisia was also the name of the wife of a famous Persian governor named Mausolus. After he died, she erected a magnificent tomb for him—one of the wonders of the ancient world. That is the derivation of our modern word mausoleum. The *artemisia* plant usually has an unhappy connotation, as well. Most Indians had no use for it. After land is overgrazed, the sage spreads rapidly, as its root toxin kills most other plants nearby. There is one encouraging note—if you stand in the smoke of a sage fire, it should dispel the evil spirits around you."

Vito snorted, not hiding his disdain. "My God," he said loudly to Lucie. "How much longer do we have to stand around here and listen to this drivel?"

She tried to shush him. "Vito, please!" Around them, the other members of the group were casting disapproving looks that would have withered most men.

"You can stay if you want to," Vito told Lucie, ignoring them. "I'm going down to the next rim viewpoint while the light's still good. You can come along when school's out."

He strode off, without giving the group or the ranger a second glance. Lucie, meeting the others' expressions with reddened cheeks, remained meekly on the outer edge of the circle.

The ranger spoke up, almost defiantly. "If there are no questions, we'll go on to the rim trail. Kindly stay together so you can hear the lecture." She moved ahead, keeping at the side of the path to let some hikers go past.

Lucie lingered at the rear of the struggling queue, still embarrassed by Vito's outburst. Afterward, she stood in dappled sunshine while the ranger pointed out the blossoms of an Indian paintbrush plant to a young couple. Lucie felt the sun warming her shoulders through her jacket and rubbed a muscle at the side of her neck, wishing she could relax and enjoy her surroundings like the others in the group. It was no use, she finally decided, as the discussion on wildflowers continued. Vito would be furious if she kept him waiting.

She grimaced apologetically as she moved on past the group and nodded her thanks to the ranger, whose expression showed what she thought of such a surrender. Lucie moved along the path, trying to look unaffected by it all, but when she turned the corner of the rim trail, she paused in relief to take in the grandeur in front of her.

Every annoyance was forgotten as she stood transfixed behind a low stone barricade, staring down into the miles of colorful limestone, sandstone, and shale ahead of her. Although the Colorado River was hidden from view in the Inner Gorge, she was able to see the tops of mountains measuring fully two thousand feet from their base alongside it. The midday sunlight faded the more vivid shades of red in the rock, but there was a complete artist's palette of other colors to be found in the fissures and crags within sight. Firs and spruce trees growing at the lower elevations provided a variation from the pines and juniper found at rim level—their green branches forming a cool and shady oasis when contrasted with the orange and brown desert colors in the rocks.

The rim path was well named, clinging precariously in places, but the Park Service had erected low stone barricades wherever there was a steep drop into the crevasse. Even so, some of the visitors showed a total disregard for safety in their efforts to get unusual camera angles or try their prowess at rock climbing. Lucie had heard the accident statistics on her first visit to the Canyon and noticed that things hadn't changed much in the interim. A few parents were letting their children run loose along the tops of the barricade, and one hiker was meditating out on a rocky spur that looked as sheer and dangerous as El Capitan. She shuddered, hoping his yoga would bring him peace of mind. He'd certainly need it, plus some luck if he was to get back on the trail unscathed.

When she rounded the next corner of the rim trail, she saw Vito taking his ease on a wooden bench near a scenic view spot. He was leaning back, with his eyes closed and his face to the sun, obviously perfecting his tan. Lucie, who had been worried that he might be angrily pacing as he waited for her, felt relief accompanied by a spurt of anger. If he'd *said* he was going to just sit around in the sun, she could have stuck with the nature lecture longer.

He must have been watching her through slitted eyes because he sat up, revealing a triumphant smile as she approached. "Ah, Lucie, *cara*," his voice was deep. "I knew you'd come."

"You made damn sure of it," she countered, not happy that he'd forced her to surrender. "I shouldn't have given in—at least not so soon. Maybe around lunchtime . . ."

He burst out laughing and patted the bench beside him. "It's a wise woman who never misses a meal. Sit down here and rest while I change film. Then I will take a magnificent picture with you in the foreground and all the color of the canyon behind you."

"I thought you'd finished taking pictures."

"Who wants strangers in a masterpiece?" He jerked his head toward a couple with backpacks who were walking slowly along the trail. He waited until they'd passed before he added, "I prefer a beautiful woman to decorate my efforts. This won't take long." He fished out a roll of film and moved to the end of the bench where there was shade. "You can tell me what you learned on the nature lecture after I left."

"I could—but I'm not going to. You behaved terribly. That poor ranger will need therapy if she meets many more men like you."

"I detest earnest young women with thick waistlines," Vito said calmly. "It doesn't matter what they're talking about."

"I should rally to the cause and feel insulted, I suppose," Lucie said, brushing the hair back from her face and watching him replace the back on his camera.

"I don't see why. You don't have a thick waist. In fact, you're not too thick anyplace. I noticed that yesterday."

Lucie opened her mouth to protest and then decided it wasn't worth the effort. Clearly Vito's thinking wouldn't be swayed. On the other hand, neither would hers—and he'd find it out the first time he made a pass. "Are we going to walk?" she asked mildly when he finally shoved the empty film box in his pocket.

"In a minute." He made no attempt to move, watching through slumbrous eyes as a family group came into view, the parents holding the hands of their two young children despite the latters' loud objections. Vito waited until they'd disappeared down the trail and then got to his feet. "I'd like you on the other side of the barricade," he announced to Lucie. "It's the only decent spot for a picture. By that tree trunk . . ."

She frowned and went over to inspect the place he'd indicated. The ground fell away sharply beyond a rocky ledge containing a twisted pine tree with straggly boughs. Lucie drew back apprehensively. "Freefall skydiving isn't my thing," she said, shaking her head.

Vito lowered the camera to stare at her. "What are you talking about? I want you next to the trunk—you can hang onto a branch if you feel uneasy. Just make sure it's behind you."

"That branch wouldn't support Chicken Little . . ."

"Who the hell's Chicken Little?" Vito had the camera up to his eye again, obviously checking the picture composition.

"Never mind." Lucie bit her lip and then moved reluctantly over to the low stone barricade at the edge of the path. "Are you sure that ledge is safe?"

"It's rock, isn't it? Of course, it's safe. Hurry up—before some Boy Scout troop comes to clutter up the landscape."

Lucie sat atop the wall, trying not to look down into the depths of the inner canyon as she put out a toe to test the pebbly surface of the narrow ledge. "I guess it's all right," she muttered.

"Just hang onto the bough," Vito instructed.

"And if the bough breaks . . ." The words of the nursery rhyme came ominously into her mind and she kept both hands on the retaining wall as she lowered her feet on the other side and gingerly shifted her weight.

"Miss Forsythe!" The call was so shrill that Lucie jerked and slithered on the pebbly rock ledge. Fortunately she was still clutching the barricade as she turned to gape at a ranger hurrying along the path toward them.

"Hell! What does *she* want?" Vito snarled after he recovered from the initial shock.

"I don't know, but I'm coming back to find out," Lucie said grimly.

It was the same woman who had been digressing so knowledgeably about *Artemisia tridentata* and Indian Paintbrush the last time Lucie had seen her. As the ranger came up, she put out a none too gentle hand to help Lucie back on the path. "The purpose of the barricade," she said disapprovingly, "is to keep visitors on *this* side. That limestone ledge is laced with cracks, and if it gave way, you'd have discovered that the bottom of the canyon is almost fifteen hundred meters below us. That translates to nearly five thousand feet." Lucie's cheeks paled visibly and the ranger softened her next words. "I'm glad I came along, Miss Forsythe."

"I had no intention of allowing such a thing to happen," Vito said, sounding more annoyed by officialdom than ever. "Did you want something special or is this another part of your lecture?"

By then, Lucie could have cheerfully pitched him over the ledge herself and just walked away. There was no reason for such rudeness merely because he'd been thwarted in his picture-taking.

The ranger chose to ignore him completely. She touched the walkie-talkie at her hip as she said, "There's an important message for you, Miss Forsythe. Whoever's calling thought you were on one of our nature walks and as soon as I heard your description, I remembered you—and your friend." Her tone made Vito sound like an appendage of doubtful value.

Lucie spoke up quickly before he could retaliate. "I can't imagine who it is. What do you want me to do? Am I supposed to phone?"

"You're supposed to report to the Visitor's Center as soon as possible," the ranger said, gesturing back down the trail.

"And would you mind telling me what I'm supposed to do?" Vito interrupted silkily.

The ranger turned to survey him, letting her glance

linger. "I'd like to," she said, "but I hope to work here for the rest of the season, so I won't. Will you follow me, Miss Forsythe?"

As the ranger started walking down the path, Lucie turned to Vito. "I don't know what this is all about," she began, only to have him shut her off with an autocratic wave of his hand.

"Go ahead," he said brusquely. "I'll be having lunch at El Tovar in half an hour. You can get in touch with me there." He turned and strode off down the rim trail in the opposite direction.

Lucie rubbed her forehead and stared after him, feeling as if she'd been caught in a whirlpool and finally dumped, sprawling, on the beach.

"Miss Forsythe?" The ranger stood waiting for her at the bend of the trail.

"Yes, I'm coming. Sorry." Lucie hurried to catch up and they made their way back to the Visitor's Center in silence. Lucie was tempted to ask the girl what she'd done with the people of her group when she'd set off and then decided it was better not to probe. After all, the ranger could have asked what Lucie saw in Vito Perelli. If the two ever met again, the accident statistics in the park would probably soar.

Her musings were cut short when she saw Paula's trim figure waiting in front of the Visitors' Center. Drew's secretary had a worried look and she was checking every tour group as it converged on the building. When her eyes lit on Lucie, a smile of relief illuminated her face and she came hurrying up.

"Thank heavens!" she said, clasping Lucie in a bear

hug and then holding her at arm's length. "I was afraid we wouldn't catch up with you."

"You mean *you're* the one who's been trying to get in touch with me?" Lucie asked incredulously.

"Well, sort of." Paula turned to smile at the ranger, who was surveying them dubiously. "It's all right. Mr. Martin knew I was going to wait out here. He can vouch for me—if you want to go in and check."

The girl nodded, obviously relieved to shelve her responsibility. "Okay, I'll go in and report to him."

Lucie watched her go and then asked Paula, "Who in the deuce is Mr. Martin?"

"The man in charge here. Come on, we're blocking traffic." Paula tugged her over to one side of the entrance where there was less confusion. "What did you do with Vito?"

Lucie looked at her watch. "He's on his way to the hotel. I have sort of a 'take it or leave it' invitation to lunch with him." She shook her head, remembering. "I thought he and the ranger were going to have a knockdown fight on the trail a few minutes ago. But what's all this about? Is something wrong? Drew isn't hurt, is he?" Her face paled as that thought occurred to her.

"No, he's fine," Paula replied. "Well, madder than a scalded cat, but now maybe he'll settle down."

"I *still* don't understand . . ."

"I know, sweetie. I'll explain on the way to El Tovar. My car's parked over here." Paula was leading the way across the lot to a yellow station wagon. "Do you suppose Vito would buy me lunch, too?" she asked as she unlocked the doors and motioned Lucie into the passenger seat.

"Of course." Lucie waited until Paula had gone around and slipped in behind the wheel before saying, "If you'd wanted to come along today, why in the world didn't you just say so? I'd have been happy for your company."

Paula laughed as she turned the ignition key. "It wasn't that—although I appreciate the thought." She checked the rear mirror before reversing and then cut competently into the main stream of traffic heading toward Hopi House and El Tovar. She turned to give Lucie a mischievous look, but her amusement faded as she saw the frown on the other's face. "What's the matter?"

Lucie's voice was flat. "When did you learn to drive? Drew told me that you didn't know how. You remember—when we were in the cottage that morning. That was the reason I brought his car south."

"I *could* say that I'd just gotten my license," Paula said after a pause.

Lucie appeared to consider it. "You could. Is it true?"

"No," Paula sighed. "You'd better read my rights."

"Loyal to the end." Lucie's lips quirked. "Why don't you just blame it on Drew? You know it was his idea."

"I refuse to testify on the grounds that—"

"All right," Lucie interrupted. "I'll take it up with Mr. McLaren the next time I see him."

"It might not be a bad idea. At least, it will give you some ammunition." Paula gave her a quick sideways glance. "He's pretty mad at you right now. At both of us, really."

"If you don't watch the road, he'll never have a chance to complain," Lucie said when the other blithely ignored the cross-traffic at an intersection leading to a park shopping center.

"You sound just like him. Probably that's why he pressed you into service when he had a chance," Paula responded, unabashed. "He wanted to protect the paintwork on his car."

"Well, it isn't any excuse for issuing orders at long distance like some kind of guru." Lucie kept her voice casual as she went on to ask, "I gather that he still isn't back home."

"Nope. He's getting closer, though. This morning he called from Flagstaff after you left." Paula managed to keep her attention on the road as they passed a park shuttle bus. "Actually he hadn't planned to talk to me at all. He transferred the call when he couldn't get an answer from your room."

"And you told him that I'd gone out with Vito?"

"Uh-huh."

"What did he say then?"

"It's a little blurred except for his opening sentence," Paula admitted. "That was 'How in the hell could you be so stupid?' After that, it got worse."

Lucie forgot about the traffic hazards and the manicured park scenery at the road's edge as she stared at Paula's profile. "Just because I was with Vito? That doesn't make sense."

Paula shrugged elegant shoulders. "I don't know whether Vito was the cause. Drew had left orders for

you to stick around. He said that didn't include tour-
ing the next county."

"He has a colossal nerve, giving orders like Attila
the Hun! I have a perfect right to go anywhere I
please."

"Don't take my head off," Paula pleaded. "Anyhow, he sent me here and contacted the rangers to try
and locate you."

"That must have taken some doing."

"Drew knows the administrative staff here," Paula
said, her explanation all the more impressive because
of its understatement.

Lucie remained adamant. "I still don't think he
needs to be so heavy-handed giving me orders."

"I know, I know. Look, he's going to phone again
this afternoon, so you can fight it out then. Right now,
I'm to keep my eye on you until we get back or I'll
lose my job."

Lucie bit her lip, realizing she'd put the secretary in
an awkward position. "I'm sorry, Paula. I didn't mean
to get you in trouble. As a matter of fact, I'll be
tickled to have you share Vito at lunch. He's too tem-
peramental for me."

The silhouette of El Tovar loomed above the road
to the right as Paula turned up a curving drive toward
it. The famed hotel with its exterior of rustic pine logs
and native boulders was situated on the very brink of
the Canyon and blended into the carefully landscaped
grounds around it.

Paula parked in a lot behind Hopi House and
walked with Lucie toward the broad, shaded porch of
the hotel. They were going through the big doors

when Paula murmured, "I hope Vito doesn't make this embarrassing. Let's tell him that I got the day off unexpectedly. That way he'll have to take pity on me."

"All right. Maybe he's left me stranded and there won't be any problem." Lucie was looking around the rustic, high-ceilinged lobby as she spoke, noting a display of Indian jewelry by the gift shop.

"No such luck. He's coming this way on an intercept course," Paula said, ostensibly attracted by a silver squash-blossom necklace. She turned deliberately and got in the first word. "Vito! I hope you've been able to make a lunch reservation. Lucie said you wouldn't mind if I joined you."

His brows came together for an instant but his expression settled into polite lines. "Of course, Paula." There was a touch of sarcasm in his voice as he turned to Lucie. "Here I was—not knowing whether to expect even one partner for lunch. Now, it appears, I'll have two."

"Thank you, Vito," Lucie said quietly, grateful that he'd apparently recovered from his annoyance. "Can we go in now?"

"Of course. They're saving a window table. There's plenty of room for the three of us." He gestured toward the dining room entrance just beyond a staircase and the reception desk.

Even in midday, the spacious dining room had a restful feeling, with oil-treated logs used for three walls and massive Indian murals decorating them. Long windows comprised the fourth wall, looking out over the Canyon with a view which was a masterpiece in itself. Indian designs in shades of brown were on the neutral carpet, blending nicely with the copper serving accessories on a buffet table in the middle of the room.

Vito exchanged a word with the maître d' and, a moment later, an extra place was being set at a choice table by the window.

When they'd ordered and the waiter had disappeared toward the kitchen, Vito leaned back in his chair. "Now, Lucie, you must tell me what happened? Did you meet Paula after your summons to the Visitors' Center?"

Since Lucie had been rehearsing her story ever since they'd entered the lobby, she was able to smile and say, "Yes—wasn't it wonderful luck! Just like the Rue de la Paix."

"Where you eventually see someone you know?" His intent regard continued. "What happened at the Visitors' Center?"

"You might as well tell him, Lucie." Paula was inspecting the cracker tray at her elbow. "He'll understand about your mother calling from Hawaii."

"Hawaii?" Vito asked incredulously.

"Yes. It was a mixup," Lucie said, trying to sound convincing. "The operator thought it was an emergency, and since it was an overseas call, the rangers put out their bloodhounds to find me. Poor Mother was just trying to find out if I was staying at one of the lodges here. Evidently the operator at McLaren's said I was at the Canyon and that started the whole thing off. I felt like an awful fool when I had to explain." She grimaced across the table. "I hope Drew doesn't hear of it or he'll think I'm not playing with a full deck."

"That's all right," Paula soothed. "He's had the same kind of trouble with me. I accused him of trying to marry me off just to get rid of me. Walter swears he offered him a bribe."

"Who's Walter?" Vito asked, clearly at a loss.

"My fiancé. He works with Drew, but he's on a business trip right now. That's why I'm footloose this afternoon." Paula sat back to let the waiter serve her soup and then went on to ask, "Did you two have anything special planned?"

"I don't know," Lucie said, happy with the apparent success of their story. She turned to look at Vito. "What do you think we should do?"

He couldn't very well say that all he wanted to do was spend the afternoon with her and obviously he knew it. His jaw was stony as he pretended to debate the options. "I think you might like to take the West Rim Drive and go out to Maricopa Point," he said finally. "Afterward we can stop for coffee and watch the mule train riders returning from their canyon ride. Is that too tame for you, Paula?"

If he had any hopes in that direction, Paula promptly squashed them. "Heavens no! It's been ages since I've been here. You know how the natives never see what the tourists do."

Vito smiled thinly and picked up his soup spoon. "Well, then—it's all settled."

"Only one thing bothers me," Paula said. "Would it be all right if we went in your car? Mine sounds awfully asthmatic these days. Walter told me to have it tuned, but I keep forgetting."

Lucie looked up, puzzled, from buttering a soda cracker. Paula's car had been running perfectly when they'd driven to El Tovar. Then as her gaze encountered the secretary's warning one, she hastily dropped her eyes. Apparently Paula didn't intend to take any more chances of getting in wrong with Drew.

Her forecast was an accurate one. For the rest of the afternoon, Paula stuck as close as a Spanish chaperone. She chattered cheerfully on the drive, oohed and aahed at the view points, drank innumerable cups of coffee as they lingered in the Bright Angel Lodge, and hung over the rail at the corral when the mule riders came wearily up from the trail. At no time did she get more than a stone's throw away from Lucie.

When it was time to head back to McLaren's, Vito walked them both to the parking lot of El Tovar and then turned to Paula, his eyes glinting. "It looks as if this is where we finally part company. Undoubtedly, we'll see you at the hotel later—probably at dinner." He broke off, seeing her disconsolate expression. "What's the matter now?"

"It's my car." She raised beseeching eyes to him. "Vito, I hate to bother you any more—but would you mind if we drove back convoy-style? That way, I wouldn't be scared if the engine cut out. It would be awful to be stuck by the roadside at this time of night."

His eyebrows came together at that. "Five-thirty is hardly the witching hour."

Lucie brought up reinforcements before he could

go on. "I know just how she feels. When I was driving
south, I always stopped early in the afternoon. A
woman alone . . ." She shook her head sorrowfully.

"I didn't know how you suffered. It doesn't matter."
There was no disguising the sarcasm in Vito's tone
then and he gestured toward the parking lot. "Get
your car, Paula. We'll follow you on the way home."

"Vito, you're a dear!" She stood on tiptoe and
aimed a kiss in the general direction of his ear. "I
won't be a minute."

"You're sure that you don't want Lucie to ride with
you," he added in mock solicitude.

"Do you think that would be better?"

"No, no. I was just teasing."

"It's a good thing," Lucie said, "because I wouldn't
be much good poking around a car's insides. Besides,
all this walking today has made me ready for a nap.
I'd hoped to doze off on the way home."

"It gets better and better," Vito said sourly. "Go
ahead, Paula, we'll follow you out of the parking lot.
After what's happened, I'll be lucky if I don't have to
change a flat for you on the way back."

With such an inauspicious beginning, the conversation between him and Lucie on the trip back was destined to be awkward. She tried a few polite comments
about the scenery but Vito had evidently decided to
sulk and finally she gave up.

Their afternoon in the fresh air must have made her
drowsier than she'd thought, because the next thing
she knew, Vito was announcing, "You'd better wake
up. We're almost at the hotel."

Lucie sat up stiffly. "Where's Paula?"

He slowed to negotiate the McLaren's curving drive leading up to the entrance. "She turned off at the other parking lot a minute ago. I didn't know you wanted to spend the evening with her, too, or I'd have stuck on her bumper. Shall I follow?"

His sardonic look was enough to make Lucie shake her head hastily. "It isn't important. You must have made good time," she added as he braked in front of the entrance.

"Not bad. Paula's car seemed to be running well—considering it was on borrowed time."

Lucie couldn't conceive an answer for that so she simply opened the door on her side and got out. "Vito—thank you for taking me today." Even as she spoke, she was trying to think of a good way to refuse a dinner invitation if he mentioned one.

She needn't have worried. Vito leaned across the seat ready to close the door as soon as she released it. "I'm happy you were able to go along, Lucie. My plans are indefinite, but there's a good chance I'll be leaving tomorrow. Otherwise—" He managed to convey his regrets with a Latin shrug.

"Of course. I hope all your plans work out. And thanks again."

He nodded and smiled, but didn't waste any time pulling the car door shut and accelerating down the drive.

Lucie let out a sigh of relief at being well out of a difficult situation. It must have been much worse for Vito, she decided with some amusement as she went across the lobby and up to her rooms. His cozy day for two had been a disaster from the beginning.

The phone started ringing as soon as she unlocked the door to the suite and she hurried across to answer it.

"Lucie?" It was a familiar feminine voice at the other end of the wire and she sank onto the edge of the telephone table in disappointment.

"Yes, Paula—I just got in. Where are you?"

"Back in the office. I wanted to make sure you'd arrived. Are you alone?"

"*Am* I? You'd better believe it. Vito would have tossed me out at the front door without even slowing down if he'd dared. And from the way he talked, he's leaving tomorrow without any regrets." She hesitated before asking casually, "Has Drew come back?"

"Nary a sign of him. Stick around, though—he hasn't left word that you're due for parole."

"He doesn't have to worry. I'm sure Vito won't be issuing any more invitations. I think he's off women for—oh, at least a day or two."

Paula's giggle came over the wire. "And I was trying to be such a discreet chaperone."

"I noticed." Lucie's tone was dry. "Actually he wasn't charmed by my company even before you arrived."

"I remember that you said he flew off the handle when the ranger came to get you."

"Even before that. He started looking disenchanted on the drive to the park—when I was quizzing him about a business acquaintance."

"You mean somebody he met en route?"

"No. It was a man he was huddling with here at the

hotel yesterday. I thought he looked familiar and mentioned it to Vito."

"Did he clear up the mystery?"

"Not really. It wasn't until this afternoon that I figured out why. I'm sure that last winter his friend came into the fur salon where I work, and bought an expensive mink."

"What's wrong with that?"

"Not a thing—except maybe his taste in women. She was a peroxide blonde who hung on his arm and called him 'lover' every three minutes. But that wasn't the reason I remembered."

Paula sounded amused. "You mean there's more?"

"There certainly was. Three days later, his picture was in the paper when he was indicted on a racketeering charge in the bay area. No wonder Vito wasn't keen on admitting who he's doing business with these days."

"I should think not." There was a sudden silence while Paula digested the facts. Then she said, "Lucie, I'll have to ring off. Someone's just come in."

"I understand. Will I see you at dinner?"

"Maybe. It's hard to tell. If you're looking for something to fill your time later on—there's a lecture on the geology of the Canyon by one of the park rangers. It's scheduled in our conference room off the lobby. I'm sure you'd enjoy it."

Her evasive answer brought a frown to Lucie's face. "I'll see how I feel when the time comes," she said, adopting the same attitude. "Well, I'll probably talk to you tomorrow."

"No doubt about it." Paula's voice became brisk

again. "And, Lucie—you will stay close. In case Drew calls and wants to speak to you."

"I'd have a hard time doing anything else tonight. G'night, Paula."

Lucie walked over by the glass door to the balcony and stared across the patio where lengthening shadows and a fiery glow at the western horizon showed that sunset wasn't long in coming. She slid the door aside and went out to sit in a lounge, deciding she might as well enjoy the spectacle. She had nothing else to do and, what was more important, no tall, stubborn hotel man to do it with.

There was sudden movement on a branch of the ponderosa pine tree close to her balcony and Lucie identified an Abert squirrel with tassel ears, gray tail, and white underparts who was looking back at her.

They stared at each other and then the squirrel's attention returned to the seed-filled cone he was holding between his paws.

Lucie's sense of humor surfaced. "Dinner? Thanks very much—I'd love to. But don't go to any trouble."

He ventured a little closer then, keeping a tight clutch on his calories.

"You're gorgeous," Lucie said in a soft monotone so he wouldn't take flight, "and your table manners are superb. It's just a pity we didn't meet earlier. By any chance," she paused hopefully, "do you play gin rummy?"

Chapter

−8−

L ucie's social schedule didn't improve as the evening wore on, but the squirrel scurried down the tree without a backward glance once he'd finished dinner.

"Just like a man," Lucie said severely as he flipped his tail and started to leave. "Don't think I won't remember this the next time you come mooching around."

She yawned then and decided she'd better look for some dinner herself before she fell asleep on the balcony. The torches which illuminated the patio were being lit down below, reminding her of a similar ceremony in a Honolulu hotel where she'd once stayed. For an instant she wished that she could go back in time to that other life without complications—when Drew McLaren hadn't become the focal point of her existence. Especially since he hadn't stayed around long enough to be notified of his nomination.

Lucie smiled ruefully as she walked through the sitting room into her bedroom, visualizing her mother's and stepfather's reactions once they knew what had happened. One thing sure, she and Drew would have to resolve their relationship before their parents arrived home.

At that moment, she would have been happy to even catch a glimpse of Drew in the distance. Paula's guarded replies about his whereabouts had caused a niggling uneasiness that was getting harder and harder to ignore.

She tried to banish her suspicions as she showered, afterward drying herself with a fluffy bath sheet before she got dressed. Deliberately she put on a georgette dress in a persimmon shade with draped cowl sleeves and a neckline that was a dramatic slash against her tanned skin. She added chunky gold earrings and nodded as she considered their effect. Even if she had to dine alone, she refused to be a forlorn, wilting figure on the sidelines. High-heeled sandals finished the illusion she was hoping to create. The looks of masculine admiration that she encountered on her walk to the dining room confirmed that she'd achieved her objective.

It was just as well she was looking her best because she was alone at the family table in the dining room, even Paula staying among the missing during the beautifully served dinner. Fortunately Vito was also missing and that aided Lucie's digestion more than anything she could buy at the pharmacy.

She soon decided, though, that no matter how delectable the dinner, nor how splendid the surroundings—it wasn't much fun unless there was someone to share it with. Someone on the same wavelength whose very presence was so exciting that—

"Oh, damn!" thought Lucie as she put down her napkin in disgust. Where in the devil was Drew?

Afterward, she was reluctant to go back to her suite and stare at the four blank walls again. Television wouldn't help her mood and, despite Paula's sales talk, she wasn't tempted by the geologic history of the Grand Canyon just then.

She wandered out through the main doors of the hotel to check the weather and decided that she'd be warm enough with her stole to take a leisurely walk through the inner patio. It was a way to pass some time and the fresh air might help her mood.

She hesitated, wondering whether to go back in the lobby and out into the patio through that door or take the curved path that followed the entrance drive and enter the walled enclosure near the parking lot.

The latter choice took longer, but she certainly had plenty of time and the quiet evening air felt almost balmy considering the season.

She flipped a mental coin and started down the outside route. The path was deserted, which wasn't surprising at that time of night; the dining room had been jammed but most of the rest of the hotel guests were happily thronging the adjoining bar or the attractive shops in the lobby.

Lucie hugged her stole around her shoulders and walked along, enjoying the insect sounds and the distinctive rattle of the yucca fronds when the breeze would freshen momentarily. She concentrated on the peaceful surroundings, carefully keeping her thoughts away from everything else, and felt her muscles relax as she neared the end of the drive.

The packed dirt walk which cut across the lawn to the patio wall wasn't lighted and she moved more carefully then. The slender heels of her shoes weren't designed for outdoor hikes of any kind, and by the time she reached the patio wall, she had accumulated a sizeable collection of grit in both sandals. She hobbled rather painfully off the path to lean against a fountain built into the wall. It was in the shadows, but she had no need of light to merely unstrap her sandals and shake out the grit.

Her movement halted abruptly as she heard angry male voices on the path behind the patio wall. They were an indistinct mumble at first, but as they came closer, the words sharpened and carried in the still air.

"I still don't know what the hell you're doing here!" It was Vito's snarling voice and Lucie instinctively moved deeper into the shadows as she heard the footsteps pull up by the nearby patio entrance. "You know what I told you to do and how to do it," Vito was ranting on. "That stuff has to be moved tonight."

"But I tell you that something's screwy about the whole setup," his companion protested. "This damn deal's been jinxed from the beginning. Ever since they loused up the first delivery date."

"I don't need you to start running my business," Vito went on coldly. "All you had to do was get out there and make sure that everything went off right."

"And be on the spot to take the rap in case anything went wrong."

"Look, you lousy bastard—nobody accuses me of double-dealing and gets away with it." Vito's tone was ominous. "Maybe you'd like to quit the operation right now."

"Vito, you know that's not what I meant . . ."

"Okay—we'll talk about it later at the payoff. Frankly, I don't give a damn what you do in the meantime. I'm going out there now and take care of things myself."

Lucie shrank back against the patio wall as the two men came through the entrance and strode down the other path toward the parking lot. When they turned the corner out of sight, she sighed with relief, aware that she'd been practically holding her breath all the time they were so close.

She stood there transfixed, trying to decide what to do next. Something rotten was afoot—there was no doubt about it. But where? That was the question.

She had to know where they were going—or, at least, the general direction, before she could even report them.

Still keeping in the shadow of the wall, she stumbled down the length of it, wishing that she'd worn other shoes when she'd started out. It would be a miracle if she didn't sprain an ankle, tramping through the flower beds.

She reached the corner of the patio just in time to see Vito's sports car reverse out of the parking lot with a squeal of tires and then head into the ghost town road at top speed. Lucie scowled as she watched, wondering what kind of delivery could be made down that deserted road. On the other hand, she told herself, a deserted road would be the very place for transfer of illegal contraband. Vito would hardly pick Interstate 66!

Her gaze fell upon Paula's station wagon parked in the nearest corner of the lot and she made a sudden decision. Damned if she was going to stand around vegetating when something was happening.

She turned and scurried back toward the hotel, hoping against hope that Drew's secretary was still somewhere around. She'd have Paula paged if she wasn't in the dining room or the lobby—or even that room where the ranger was lecturing. That might be the best place to start looking.

As soon as she hurried through the doors into the lobby, she saw that luck was with her. Paula was standing by the registration desk talking to a uniformed hotel security guard.

Lucie's frantic dash had left visible traces in her muddied sandals and breathless appearance. Paula gave her a startled look as soon as she came through the door and started over to meet her.

"Lucie! What in the world's happened? Are you all right?"

Lucie waved that aside. "Of course," she said, trying to catch her breath. "Paula, can I borrow your car keys? Right away."

"Well, I guess so." Paula's fingers went automatically toward her purse. It wasn't until she had the keys halfway out of her bag that she hesitated. "What are you going to do?"

"Go for a drive," Lucie said tersely, reaching over and taking them from her. "Paula—that guard over there . . ." She nodded toward the man who was ob-

serving them even as he relaxed against the registration desk, one hand resting on the walkie-talkie at his
belt.

"What about him?" Paula asked sharply.

"Can he get in touch with the highway patrol or
whoever's in charge of things?"

"Of course. So can I. Lucie—what's going on?"

"Keep your voice down," Lucie advised. "I don't
know what this is about except that Vito's in it up to
his neck and it's happening on the road to the ghost
town." She ignored Paula's swift indrawn breath and
started for the door then, saying over her shoulder,
"I'll stay on the fringes, so you don't have to worry."

Paula took a quick step after her and then drew up.
"Damn it all!" she said with feeling before she hurried
over toward the guard. "Come on, Fred. You'll have
to get in touch with Drew fast or he'll have our hide."

When Lucie reached the parking lot she was so out
of breath that she could hardly manage to unlock the
door of Paula's car and fall onto the seat.

It took more time for her nervous fingers to find the
slot for the ignition key, and after that, she wasted
precious moments looking for the headlight switch
and brake release. Her struggles, compounded with
her dash to the parking lot, left her visibly trembling
as she finally turned the car out onto the road.

She'd passed the well-lighted outbuildings of the
resort almost before she knew it and suddenly was
into the unrelieved darkness of the stark plateau land
beyond.

Only a city person would realize exactly *how* dark
it was, Lucie thought uneasily, as the headlights of

Paula's car bored a thin shaft through the gloom on the deserted road.

Lucie lifted her foot from the accelerator and suddenly let the car's speed slacken, as she remembered that Vito and his accomplice hadn't said *where* on the road their transfer would take place. There might be all kinds of turnoffs on either side of the car. Lucie frowned as she tried to remember from their drive in the daylight. If only she'd been paying more attention!

As the car idled along, she became conscious that not only was the road completely without illumination—it also was apparently devoid of traffic. It was impossible for her to recall just then if the road ended at the ghost town junction or whether it continued. If it ended at the old town, the absence of local traffic wasn't surprising. Lucie's expression was thoughtful as she considered it. A deserted road and deserted buildings made a perfect combination for illicit dealings.

For the first time, it occurred to her that even if she parked down by the turnoff to the ghost town, her presence would be speedily noted by any intruders. Of course, she could turn off the headlights and coast along to a vantage spot on the road—the way they did in the movies. Her lips twisted wryly even as she thought about it. That was easier said than done. On unfamiliar terrain in the inky darkness, she'd be off the road and stuck in the soft, sandy shoulder before she'd gone a car length!

That realization made her slow even more and she was forced to acknowledge that she'd been too impulsive again. Only this time it might prove disastrous.

She would have attempted a U-turn but the same

hazards accompanied that as coasting without lights. Paula's car wasn't a compact and the two-lane road wasn't wide. Glimpses of the shoulders showed they were still mainly sand—which could be calamitous if her wheels settled in it. There was only one thing as bad as arriving unexpectedly at Vito's rendezvous, and that was being stuck on the roadside for him to discover later.

When she'd considered all the possibilities, she decided her best chance would be to turn around at the ghost town spur—where the workmen had been erecting the stone entrance. Even if Vito was conducting his business along Main Street, he might think the car belonged to a motorist who'd just taken the wrong road, and allow her to drive off unmolested. It didn't sound like a very good solution, but it was possible.

Lucie continued to drive carefully, keeping a sharp eye for lights at the side of the road. Fortunately, Paula's car was running well, so she didn't have to worry in that regard. As she drove, she had time to reconsider Drew's order for her to stay close to the resort. In view of what she'd just overheard, it was possible he'd suspected something dangerous was taking place on McLaren land. If so, then hopefully Paula and the security man had contacted him. He might even be following on the road.

Her anxious glance went to the rear view mirror of the car, hoping that some headlights might be materializing even then in the blackness of the night. Her lips compressed as she observed that no miracles had occurred; the road she'd just traveled was still dark and deserted. When her eyes moved down to the windshield again, concentrating on the scene ahead, she saw that a definite change had taken place in the landscape. A subdued glow of illumination rose like an aureole over the ghost town relics on the hillside to the right of the highway.

Lucie reacted as if she'd received a sharp blow in the stomach. It was one thing to overhear disjointed threats and conversation in the middle of civilization and quite another to have them confirmed in the middle of nowhere.

She braked slightly as she neared the turnoff, trying to peer through the half-light on the hillside and see what was going on. There was the outline of what appered to be a good-sized truck in the middle of the town's main street, and two or three figures moved in and out of the shadows even as she watched. All activity centered near the tailgate of the truck, and Lucie muttered, "They're unloading something," unaware that she'd even spoken aloud.

Her sense of foreboding deepened as a "Dead End Road" sign loomed before the headlights. That settled the question of whether or not she could drive on past. It also committed her to the original course of turning around in the narrow cutoff which suddenly became visible in front of her car.

The stonemasons had accomplished a great deal since she'd last seen the entrance and she wondered irrelevantly if Vito was aware of their progress. For it *was* Vito and his sidekicks up on the hillside—she was as sure of it as if she'd seen them under a strong floodlight, The same instinct told her that he would show no mercy to anyone who got in his way.

Her foot pushed down hard on the brake as she turned into the ghost town cutoff. She had to manage a smooth turnaround that didn't waste any time, but didn't give the impression of furtive panic, either.

It went against every impulse in her. At that moment when she was stopped, every nerve ending she possessed protested. Her hands shook as she reached for Paula's gearshift and she could have screamed when she killed the engine trying to go into reverse.

A searchlight suddenly flashed from the truck on the hillside and Lucie automatically cut her own lights as she saw the searchlight beam hone down toward her car.

She felt panic creep up her like an icy tide and tried to ignore it as she bent desperately to the ignition switch.

Suddenly the car door beside her was ripped open. "Move over," ordered a ruthless male voice.

As she froze terror-stricken on the seat, the intruder implemented his command by grasping her around the waist and shoving her to the other side of the car as he threw himself behind the wheel. "Now follow my lead or you'll get us both killed," he growled.

By then, Lucie was only conscious of one thing and she sagged on the seat like a puppet without strings. "Damn you, Drew McLaren," she hissed. "I could murder you myself. You've taken five years off my life."

His hands tightened so hard on her waist that she gasped. "You'll be lucky to have five more years," he muttered. "Now shut up and put your arms around my neck!"

"Here?" She was incredulous. "Are you out of your mind?"

Drew shoved her down across the seat, almost smothering her as he fell on top. "We're about to have company," he warned in her ear. "Play along with me—or it might be a final performance!"

Chapter

–9–

The next few minutes were mostly a confusing blur, although a part of Lucie's mind seemed to be functioning as an impartial observer. She knew when Vito's lookout man appeared beside the car door by Drew's reaction. Her stricken gasp must have been convincing because she heard a rough laugh and then a male voice jeer, "God—wouldn't you know! Two lovebirds!" as a flashlight beam illuminated the car's interior.

Drew kept his head lowered but managed an offended sputter about, "It's still a free country.'

"Not here, sonny. Take your girl friend and get the hell out of here—while you still can," came the immediate retort.

"I will, if you'll turn off that damned light," Drew said, sounding resentful.

"Look, buddy—I give the orders." The man beside the car took his time about droppng the flashlight beam to the side of the car. "Now get that heap turned around before my boss comes down with another idea."

Drew made a project of sitting upright. "Can't you

172

give us a minute? It'll take that long to find my keys—then we'll go. I don't know why you're so teed off. There's plenty of unoccupied space around here."

"Then go claim your squatters' rights." The guard had clearly lost interest in them. "If I don't see your back bumper going down the road in about two minutes . . ."

"I get the idea," Drew cut in. He turned his attention to Lucie still huddled along the seat. "C'mon, doll—pull yourself together. Where did you put those keys? Next time, you can keep your hands off of them unless . . ." He broke off as he heard a disgusted snort from the man outside the car and then his retreating footsteps. Immediately Drew's voice changed. "I think we're out of the woods," he said in a tense undertone as he turned Paula's key in the ignition and started the engine.

Lucie was trying to pull her clothes into order as she sat up. "Where did you find it?" she asked in a muffled voice.

"Find what?"

"The key. You told him that I had it."

"It was in the car all the time. I had to say something. We couldn't very well talk about the weather." Drew was reversing as he spoke, turning back down the road toward the resort. "Now the thing is to get out of here before we attract any more attention up on the hill."

"But that's what I came to see." Reality was setting in again and Lucie straightened indignantly. "That's Vito up there—I'm sure of it. And he's doing something crooked . . ."

"I know."

"I tried to tell Paula," Lucie continued. "And she was supposed to get in touch with the authorities, but if they don't hurry—" She stopped almost in midsyllable to do a double take. "*What* did you say?"

"That we've had the town staked out for the past two days." Drew was speaking rapidly as he let the car ease along. "Then you come and almost louse up the whole operation. I should put you in a straitjacket."

"You can't." Lucie's voice sounded numb.

"Give me one good reason—"

"I didn't keep up my payments on it."

Drew let out a groan. "A comic yet. My god! You could have gotten yourself killed back there."

Lucie flounced on the seat, adjusting her dress. "I knew I was in trouble but murder wasn't the only thing I was worried about. You certainly threw yourself into your part." There was a wary undertone to her words.

"How do you think people act when they're necking in a car?"

"I really couldn't say."

Her cool tone got through to him. "I'm not sure of the finer details myself," he said not too convincingly, "but I have a good imagination. I was sorry to put you through such an experience. I knew you were nervous—I felt you stiffen in my arms when that goon appeared."

"He wasn't entirely responsible for my reaction," she said with dignity. Then she drew in her breath when Drew suddenly turned off the headlights and braked, opening the door beside him as the car stopped. "Where are you going now?" she wailed.

"To rejoin the others. Slide behind the wheel—c'mon, hurry!" He waited for her to slip over to the driver's seat before he reached to the dash and turned on the lights again. "Now—drive like the devil back to the hotel and stay there. We'll make sure you aren't followed."

Her eyes were wide and anxious in the dim light. "Drew—be careful."

"I will." He winked, pushed the door closed with a barely audible sound and disappeared into the darkness beyond the roadside.

Lucie stared unhappily after him and then, remembering his terse instructions, put her foot down on the accelerator and kept it there.

There wasn't any traffic on the road until she reached the lights of the resort later—probably because there was a sedan with two security men in it parked at the boundary of the hotel grounds. She drew a breath of relief as the curving drive finally came into view, not realizing until then that reaction was setting in.

Lucie decided to park in the well-lighted drive of the hotel rather than the shadowy lot. She pulled the car into the loading zone and gave the keys to a surprised bellman when she got out. "Would you see that Mrs. Bennett gets them, please."

"Of course, Miss Forsythe." It was the bellman who had taken her to the room when she'd arrived. "Will you be needing the car any more tonight?"

Lucie barely restrained a shudder, remembering the

drama still being staged out on that stark hillside. "No, I'll be in for the rest of the evening."

She gave the same message to the switchboard operator when she reached her room and found the desk calling.

The operator made a note of it before saying, "Mrs. Bennett asked to be notified. I'm not sure where to locate her just now, Miss Forsythe. Shall I have her call?"

"There's no need. I'll get in touch with her tomorrow. Just tell her that everything's all right."

Lucie caught sight of her reflection in an antiqued wall mirror then and shuddered. The way she looked, it was time for a bath and a complete change.

Her clothes were shed without ceremony while she was running the water. She bundled them unceremoniously, starting to put them in the hamper before she stopped in her tracks. "Don't be a ninny," she said aloud—but went over to the basket and lifted the cover the barest amount possible to make sure it was empty. Drew was right about that straitjacket, she thought in resignation after she tossed her laundry in. One more night like this, and she'd be shopping for it in the catalog.

For one so far gone, Lucie showed considerable thought in selecting a fragrant jasmine bubble bath and pouring in a lavish amount.

She stayed in the tub long enough to wash away all reminders of her night's adventures but emerged from the water in a far shorter time than was her usual custom, remembering the proverb that "Once is a mistake—twice is a habit." She resolved that from then on, Drew would be received only in the sitting room.

She finished toweling herself dry and put on a floor-length leisure gown of a silky aqua jacquard. It was a wraparound with a slash neckline descending almost to the obi-sashed waist; a style that was severely simple but beautifully executed. She dabbed a discreet amount of Patou's Supreme Moment behind her ears and then, after hesitating, in the shadowed hollow of her breasts. She didn't bother to look in the mirror after that, knowing that her flushed cheeks were a dead giveaway as to the trend of her thoughts.

Resolutely, she walked out of the sitting room of the suite and moved over to the balcony to stare down upon the hotel's inner patio. The wrought iron torches burned brightly around the perimeter of the tiled pool, since the faint stirring of breeze was barely strong enough to bend the flames. A crescent of moon came into view briefly as the thin cloud cover parted and then converged again like a curtain on the night.

It was such a peaceful and quiet scene that it was hard to comprehend what was occurring on that hillside. Lucie closed her eyes tightly, visualizing all the things that could be happening to Drew at that moment. Her murmured entreaty of "Let him be all right," showed how vulnerable she was, as well.

The waiting seemed easier to bear after that and Lucie lost track of time while she stood there, carefully keeping her mind blank as she savored her pleasant surroundings. It was hard to imagine a more peaceful and enjoyable place to live. If only—and then she clamped down on her wandering thoughts

again before she dared dream about what her future
might hold.

She turned back into the sitting room, switching off
the overhead light and turning on a lamp atop the
record console against the wall. There was a chair
close by, but Lucie ignored it, sitting on the floor in
front of the stereo to inspect the record shelves and
tape storage boxes.

She put on Debussy's *La Mer* and was admiring the
record jacket on some Chopin waltzes when she heard
footsteps coming down the hall from Drew's bedroom.
Startled, she looked up to see him on the threshold
and then dropped her eyes in confusion as his own
glance wandered deliberately over her seated figure.

The soft lamplight caught the gleaming highlights
in her hair, giving her an ethereal quality that made
him say gruffly, "You remind me of that famous mer-
maid statue in Copenhagen. Poised and waiting to
take on all comers." He bestowed a slow grin on her
as he came on into the room. "No, don't get up—I'll
sit in this chair."

"If I remember, that statue wasn't overdressed,"
Lucie replied, trying to keep her voice casual to offset
the color in her cheeks.

"How about a Lorelei then, luring unsuspecting
men to their doom?"

"You're remarkably poetic—considering the circumstances." She could continue the nonsense because
he obviously had come through the troubles unscathed. His hair was still damp from a shower, and
somewhere along the line, he'd changed into flannel
slacks and a clean shirt. The sleeves were rolled up to

his forearms and he'd unbuttoned it at the throat. "I didn't know you were even back," she said.

"You mean this?" His gesture took in his clean garb. "I changed at the office. Dad and I keep some extra clothes there. The police wanted a statement from me after it was all over and it seemed easier to kill two birds—in a manner of speaking."

Lucie bit her lip. "Not literally?"

"No way. Vito will probably be out of custody as soon as he can get hold of his lawyer. I have an idea he'll be screaming about his rights all the way to Phoenix. By then, he'll even have a reason for a cache of illegal arms and ammunition." Drew sighed and stretched long legs out on either side of Lucie's seated figure.

She carefully kept from touching him, but she made no effort to move away. "It *was* Vito's operation then? I wasn't hearing things by the patio?"

"No, you weren't hearing things." He leaned forward to flick the lobe of her ear with his forefinger. "Nevertheless, grandma—next time there's something going on, make damned sure you keep those big ears out of things."

"They *aren't* big," she felt impelled to protest.

"No, they're not. But that's another story, so you can stop fishing," he announced blandly. "How about fetching us a glass of something tall and cold while I'm getting my strength back. There should be a selection in the refrigerator over there."

"If I weren't a free-loading guest, I wouldn't be so obliging," she said lightly, taking care to avoid touching his flannel-covered thigh as she got to her feet. "Did you ever have any dinner?"

"I forgot all about it. Never mind, we can send down for sandwiches later—if we remember."

The latter part of his comment registered but she ignored the teasing gleam in his eyes, pretending to survey the contents of the refrigerator. "*Arancia, birra, coca*?" she announced in the singsong of an Italian street vendor. "What's your pleasure?"

"Whatever's handiest—just so it's wet."

She nodded and handed him an iced soft drink in a tall glass and then went back to squeeze lime in a glass of tonic water for herself. She stayed prudently by the bar to drink it, watching as Drew took a long swallow before he cradled the glass between his palms.

"You were telling about Vito," she prompted. "How long have you known what was going on up there?"

"Not long enough. I knew that he'd dabbled in some questionable activities in his time, but I still didn't tumble as to why he spent so much time here. He got a little careless toward the end—too many of his business associates had criminal records."

"Then I wasn't the only one who recognized his 'associate' the other day?"

"Apparently not. How did you happen to be acquainted with him?" Drew asked in a careful tone.

Lucie's shoulders shook with laughter. "If you could only see your face," she said finally, wiping the corners of her eyes. "And such a diplomatic approach . . ."

"Careful, love, you're treading on the flypaper. Better give me a straight answer while you can. Otherwise . . ." He left it dangling.

Lucie had no intention of allowing him to get off so easily. "Actually it was a business relationship. I thought Paula had told you. It concerned a mink coat," she went on when Drew simply waited. "He bought it in our salon for a friend of his who came along that day. She was so—colorful—that she tended to put him in the shade."

"Probably a woman of many talents," Drew said gravely.

"I'm sure of it," she matched his tone. "When a woman can convince a man to pay cash on the line for a floor-length ranch mink, that's talent."

"Ummm. I'll remember."

"Yes—well, I wish I had. Earlier, I mean. Then I wouldn't have thrown a wrench in the works tonight. Of course," she concentrated on her frosty glass, "it would have been nice if you'd told me what was going on. Instead of acting like the Invisible Man."

"I didn't mean to beat such a fast retreat," Drew confessed. "But I've learned that being around you poses a certain inherent danger." He grinned, "I've found I have this irresistible urge to make love to you."

"I see," she said, trying to sound equally nonchalant and not succeeding very well.

"No, you don't—but you will." He went on without a pause, "Anyhow, as soon as I got in my office, I received a call from the federal authorities in Phoenix. They'd just been tipped off on this transfer tonight.

They'd heard about the operation before this, but never pinpointed a location. It seems Vito and his friends had been using Canyon Hill for over six months."

"But what were they shipping?"

"Arms, ammunition, drugs. We're not far from the Mexican border, so it was damned convenient. The ghost town was ideal for their setup. Drive an occasional truck through in the middle of the night—unload the cargo . . ."

"But where?"

"A ready-made cache. The old boarded-over reservoir. Only they remodeled it slightly to make things easier. After they stored their merchandise, all they had to do was sift some sand and rock across the top and wait until they scheduled a pickup. Even the weather obliged in this part of the country."

"No wonder Vito didn't want you messing around with the ghost town. I thought he was a little paranoid on the subject at the time."

Drew nodded and took a final swallow of his drink. "Paranoid is the right adjective. I think he's the one who tried to discourage me up in Jackson. The police there have arrested a parole violator who's claiming that he was hired for a hit and run setup. We'll see what develops." Drew nodded his thanks as Lucie came to collect his glass and take it back to the bar counter.

"I suppose he thought that if he could put you out of commission for a few months, it would help," she commented.

"He does seem given to sudden impulses," Drew said with some irony.

"He must have had another one today at the canyon. Before Paula arrived."

"What are you talking about?" Drew's eyebrows came together.

"Well, I'd been asking questions about his sidekick and that was the last thing he wanted just then. If he could have arranged an accident on that ledge by the trail—" She broke off to protest, "Don't look like that, Drew. It wasn't even close. The ranger arrived then and he couldn't do anything about her. Poor Vito!" Lucie gave a lowpitched laugh. "He had a terrible day. I could almost feel sorry for him if he wasn't such a conceited toad."

"Well, don't start suffering unduly. He'll be out on bail before morning—probably starting his parlor tricks all over again. But at least not in this hotel. He can stow rattlesnakes someplace else from now on."

"I'd forgotten about that," Lucie said in such a tone of indignation that Drew doubled with laughter. "I certainly don't see anything funny about it."

"There wasn't at the time—but looking back on it now," he said judiciously, "it did have its moments."

Lucie had a very good idea of the very moment he was talking about. She tried to ignore the surge of red flooding her face as she said, "I discovered that Vito wasn't the only one trying parlor tricks. For a beginner, Paula drives very well. She managed all the way to the park today by herself. You'd better cringe," she added severely, "after using such a dodge to get me here."

"I had to do it." Drew spoke as if his action didn't even need defending. "At the time, I wasn't exactly sure why. Now I am."

"I see."

"You keep saying that." As the Debussy clicked off, he gestured toward the record console. "I liked your choice. What's next?"

Lucie succumbed to the diversion. "I was thinking of Chopin—if that's all right. He seems to fit the mood." Walking across the room, she retrieved the album from the floor and put some records on the player. No sooner had she finished than she found Drew's long legs stretched out to bar her escape.

"Sit down—where you were before," he commanded, his voice low and deliberate. "Within reach."

If she'd protested, it would have been silly, since that was exactly where she wanted to be. For appearances' sake, she said mildly, "You have a penchant for ordering me around," even as she obediently curled on the rug in front of his chair.

"That's where you're wrong. It's the end result that counts—not the execution."

Her eyebrows climbed. "Which means?"

"I like to have you in my arms." There was no laughter in his tone then. "That's what I discovered that first day by the corral. Even keeping away from you that night in the cottage was damned difficult."

"You did a good job." Lucie's voice was unsteady as she felt his hands come to rest on her shoulders and then move caressingly down. "I thought you played the big brother role to perfection."

"Well, forget it. I've changed the order of things.

You've been cast for a different part from now on."
His voice was rough as he bent to nuzzle her ear.

Lucie's heart beat so hard that it was difficult for
her to answer. She turned to look up at him. "You
don't want a sister?" she asked in a husky little
whisper.

He moved to kiss her. "Hardly," he murmured, his
lips barely touching hers. "But I'll take a wife."

As the kiss deepened, he slid down from the chair
and Lucie felt the hard length of his body come down
beside her on the rug. Then she forgot everything but
Drew's possessive touch on her skin as his lips moved
to explore and capture.

It was the record finally finishing on the player
above them which brought them back to bemused reality. Drew pulled away just far enough to prop on an
elbow and smile down on Lucie, savoring her love-
liness. A tiny pulse beat in her throat and he bent to
kiss it, letting his lips follow the deep slash neckline of
her gown.

Lucie quivered as his exploration broadened. "I
thought you were going to be sensible," she said, trying to sound severe. "After all, we're not in the front
seat of a car now."

"Ummm." His hand settled the neckline back into
place, taking more care than necessity demanded. "It's
a pity. I discovered tonight that I'd been missing
something all these years."

"I can't think what," she said, capturing his fingers
and pressing a kiss on them to soften the restriction.
"You're entirely too proficient."

"I'll be better with practice," he grinned. "That reminds me. I thought we might let Paula and Walter run this place for a week or so while we fly to Hawaii and invite your mother and my father to our wedding. Afterward, we'll leave them in peace on Oahu and pick our own island for a honeymoon. Does that sound good?"

"Darling Drew." Her palms cradled his head. "It sounds heavenly!"

"That's settled then." His lips brushed hers before he added, "There's a ranch on the big island of Hawaii—with a wonderful string of saddle horses. You'll love the place." He started to chuckle at her chagrined expression and then, a moment later, their shared laughter faded as awareness and desire replaced it.

"Lucie, love—" Drew's arms tightened around her almost painfully—"the place doesn't matter. Just so you're with me for the rest of our lives."

Her voice was warm with happiness and rich with promise. "Now and forevermore?"

"Absolutely. Strictly a family affair," he said and put his mouth demandingly on hers.